Playing Basra

Playing Basra

Edward Brown

Exile Editions

Publishers of singular
Fiction, Poetry, Drama, Non-fiction and Graphic Books
2008

Library and Archives Canada Cataloguing in Publication

Brown, Edward, 1969-
    Playing Basra / Edward Brown.

ISBN 978-1-55096-113-3

    I. Title.

PS8603.R68318P53 2008   C813'.6   C2008-905969-7

Design and Composition by Active Design Haus
Typeset in Garamond and Century Gothic fonts at
    the Moons of Jupiter Studios
Cover photo by G. Baden/zefa/Corbis
Printed in Canada by Gauvin Imprimerie

The publisher would like to acknowledge the financial assistance of
the Canada Council for the Arts and the Ontario Arts Council, which is an
agency of the Government of Ontario.

  Conseil des Arts **Canada Council**
                       du Canada   for the Arts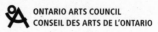

Published in Canada in 2008 by Exile Editions Ltd.
144483 Southgate Road 14
General Delivery
Holstein, Ontario, N0G 2A0
info@exileeditions.com
www.ExileEditions.com

Canadian Sales Distribution: U.S. Sales Distribution:
McArthur & Company   Independent Publishers Group
c/o Harper Collins   814 North Franklin Street
1995 Markham Road   Chicago, IL 60610
Toronto, ON M1B 5M8   www.ipgbook.com
toll free: 1 800 387 0117   toll free: 1 800 888 4741

For Rebecca, for your advice on writing.

IN A ROOM
ABOVE A VARIETY STORE

My brother Donny needed a haircut. Last time I was by, I had promised him I'd come after school in a few days and give him a trim. I teach third grade. On Wednesday by four, I'm at his place.

For years, Donny had been cutting his own hair. Made a mess of it. Eventually, he stopped and it grew in. It became tangled, matted. Couldn't get a comb through it. Impossible to keep clean.

One day, out of the blue, he asked me if I'd cut it for him. That first time hadn't been easy. The scissors were dull. The room was dark. The only light came from the glow of the TV set which Donny never turned off, and the small amount of daylight that came in though the window. His hair had become so tangled, I had to cut most of it off.

Since then, I've cut Donny's hair every couple of weeks. Usually, just a trim. Off the collar. Keep it neat. His thick brown hair grows back fast. When I'm done, it doesn't look so good, chopped and uneven. I tell Donny, if the lighting was better and the scissors were sharper, I could do a better job.

"Don, can I at least turn the table lamp on?"

He tells me, "No." He won't let me use any other scissors. These ones were Ma's. They're the ones he likes.

When I'm through, Donny's always happy with the haircut. That's all that matters.

Donny gets by on a Canadian Forces disability pension. Seven hundred and eighty dollars a month. Except for doctors' appointments, Donny hasn't been out of his room in seven years. I do little things for him, like cut his hair, bring him groceries, remind him to bathe. I do his laundry. Pick up his prescriptions. Help him keep the bills paid.

He's forty-six years old and lives alone in a rented room above a variety store.

Donny sleeps on a cot in the corner. Every morning he makes his bed. He likes things neat. Ma was like that, too. No clutter. No books or photographs. The bathroom needs renovating. The faucets are old. There's rust in the sink and in the tub where the water has dripped. The entire place needs a paint job. Donny keeps the room so dark, I can't even tell what colour the walls are. The only light is the lamp on the table by the window where Donny builds his model cars. They're detailed, so he needs good light when he's working on them. Weeks go into each one, and then after he's assembled them, they're placed back in the Revell box they came in. Right now, he's working on a cerulean blue '66 Chevy II. When he's done that one, I'll get him something else.

We cut his hair in the part of the room where the floor is tiled. It's too small to be called a kitchen. The room came with an apartment-sized refrigerator, a hotplate, a microwave, and a tiny bar-sink. It's cramped. It would be better to cut his hair closer to the window, but Donny said on the vinyl tile, hair was easier to sweep up. Donny sits on a stool I bought at a garage sale. The entire time

I'm cutting, he keeps his eyes closed and barely says a word. Donny's tall. So that he'd be at the right level, I had to saw the legs down.

With a towel across his shoulders, I begin at the back. The scissors are ice cold, chilled. Donny thinks scissors cut better when they're not warm. I don't know how he came to believe this. It isn't true. Still, a few hours before I get here, he'll take the scissors out of the junk drawer and place them in the freezer.

Our lives are different. I have my own family, a house, work as a teacher. Donny has a rented room and stacks of model cars in boxes. It took longer than it should have, but eventually, I finished university. In my last year, Janice got pregnant. By then, we were renting an apartment on Dawes Road. I had to work full-time and complete my degree at night. Two months after Alison was born, Janice and I got married.

Things were okay until Ma got sick and had to go into the hospital. Around the same time, Ray, my other brother, split. Until Ma was hospitalized, Donny had been living with her. Now that she was sick, he couldn't cover the rent. He got evicted.

After that, Donny lost it completely. Lived on the street. Got roughed up by police, by security guards. He got arrested a few times. Ended up in the Queen Street psyche ward.

When I'm cutting around the front, the scissors close to his face, Donny closes his eyes tighter. His eyebrows bunch together. The flesh at his temples creases.

"Relax," I tell him. "When you do that, it makes your hair uneven."

He doesn't want me to talk. With his eyes still closed, he responds, "Just get it done."

I comb a length of hair, hold it between my fingers, cut. Dry hairs fall away, covering the towel, the floor around our feet.

Every time we do this, I'll tell him, "Don, hair's easier to cut when it's wet."

I've tried using a spray bottle to dampen the hair a little. He doesn't even like that. He's got this fear about getting his head wet. I've given up trying to convince him to shower. He prefers bathing with a facecloth and a bowl of soapy water.

I lean away from him to see if I'm cutting straight. It's hard to really tell.

"Don't worry," Donny told me, "just cut."

In the spring of 1990, Janice and I bought a house not far from where I grew up. Moved in. Fixed it up. Got settled. Three years later, Janice was pregnant again. Another girl. I've been lucky that way.

We live close enough to walk to Donny's. His room is above Parks Variety. The Park family is Korean. They run the store. They own the building. They realize Donny's sick, but they're good to him, anyway. Every morning, Mr. Park or one of his boys checks on Donny. If anything's up, they'll call me. Donny prepares his own food. Still, Mrs. Park insists on taking him up a bowl of steamed rice for lunch. Sometimes, she'll bring him fish. For his part, Donny's quiet. He doesn't cause trouble. He spends his days watching TV or making model cars. The building has cockroaches, mice. Donny doesn't complain. Because the Parks are kind to my brother, I don't say anything, either.

I try to get Donny's hair even on both sides. Taking him by the chin, I turn his head, side to side. Even now, after all he's been through, Donny's still strong. He's a full head taller than either Ray or me, and both of us are around five-eight or five-nine. He's solid through the chest, wide across the shoulders.

Below us, someone entered the store. I hear Korean. Mr. Park laughs. The cash register springs open.

I take my brother's face, gentle with my hand, moving it at will. Allowing me to do this, his head pivots like a machine. I pause to study him. With his chin rough with stubble, flesh grey and creased, he looks older than he really is.

To me, Donny's like a machine, made up of working parts, functional, but never entirely whole. He wasn't always this way. A long time ago parts of Donny were torn out. Over time, something like steel, hard, impenetrable filled the empty space inside him. It took years for me to realize that the surviving parts of Donny served one purpose, that of keeping us together, assembling us into a family.

When Donny's hair looked about even on both sides, I cut around the top. There's a game show on the TV. The volume is low. When they go to a commercial, I can hear music, applause.

Eyes still closed, Donny grins, "You better not be givin' me a bowl cut."

"Sorry, Don. I'm a teacher, not a barber. The bowl cut's the only cut I know."

School keeps me busy, but I try to visit Donny as often as I can. I'll stop in on the way home or go over on a Saturday. I used to bring the girls along for a visit. Then Janice told me they don't want to go. She said I was forcing them.

I asked her why she thought they didn't want to go.

"They told me," she said.

"Oh."

Alison said the scars up and down Donny's arms were scary. Catherine said where their uncle lived was dark and smelled bad.

When we'd go there, the girls would stand behind me, cowering. Especially the little one. Sooner or later, they'd come around. They'd say hi, smile, not much else.

At times, Donny seemed nervous in their company. Sometimes he would talk to them. Other times, he wouldn't.

I argued with Janice, "I'm not forcing them to go." At the time, Alison was seven. Catherine was four. When I look back now, it was pretty obvious that they were afraid of their uncle. It was in their faces. The apprehension before we'd start up the narrow staircase that led to his room. I'd kneel, look them in the eyes, stressing how important these visits were.

"Your uncle's sick, but he's okay."

Alison would ask, "What's he got?"

I'd answer, "He's got—" Then I'd be stuck. I'd just tell them, "He's been through a lot."

One Saturday, as we were leaving for Donny's, I told them, if they really didn't want to go, they didn't have to. We were outside already, on the sidewalk. I was hoping to prove Janice wrong, I was hoping they'd say that they really wanted to visit their uncle. Instead, they handed me the drawings they had made for Donny.

In a little voice, Catherine said, "Say *hi* to Uncle Donny." She followed her big sister up the steps, onto the porch and back into the house.

Donny still has all the pictures they've drawn for him. When there was no more room left on the refrigerator door to display them, he taped them to the walls.

Donny goes through phases where he'll eat a lot of the same thing. For days, he'll only drink warm water. Every single day for two weeks straight, he'll eat Kraft Dinner and canned beets. Next thing, it'll be fruit. Oranges, he likes those in particular. I'll pick up two or three from some little market along the Danforth. We'll share an orange and watch some of a TV show. Sometimes we'll talk. I'll tell him about work, about one of my students. He'll tell me about the model he's working on. Other times, he'll say he just wants to be quiet.

The room's always dark, stuffy. Donny said that's how he liked it. When I first arrive, I'll open the blinds, telling him, he's got to let daylight in. When the weather's good, I try to coax him outside. Outside would be good for Donny. Withrow Park is a block away. We could sit on a bench. Pet dogs. Watch squirrels.

For a while now, I've been trying to convince him to get a plant. I've told him, one of these times I'm going to bring him one.

Slowly getting up from his shabby recliner, he'll pull the blinds back down.

"I don't wanna go out. I wanna stay in," he'll tell me, then he'll chuckle the way he's always chuckled, a dry stutter, mechanical, like an engine before it stalls.

"Mikey," he sighed, "what the fuck do I want with a plant?"

I laughed. "I don't know."

Donny's the only one who calls me Mikey anymore. Now it's Michael, now it's Mr. Hogan. When he does, for a second we're young, we're boys again. I like the way it makes me feel. At the same time, I hate the feeling.

I comb Donny's hair. Trim the back more. Straighten the bangs. When his hair's done, I tell him not to move. "Let me sweep up first." He obeys.

With a dustpan and a broom, I sweep around his slippers. The entire time, his eyes stay closed. After a minute, he touches his hair with both hands.

Crouching, I ask, "You want to see what it looks like? I'll turn the lamp on. Let me get a mirror."

"No. Don't worry. It's good."

I've never told Janice this, but what I've always wanted is for Donny to live with us. We've got room. It'll never happen, so I never bring it up. Janice, the girls and me, we're all Donny's got. Ma's dead. Ray's out west. Alberta, I think. Last time Ma, Ray, Donny and I were all together was the Christmas Alison was a baby. Ma was sick already. We did Christmas at our place. They let her out for the holiday. Ray came in on a Greyhound bus. At breakfast the next morning, he said he was starting a new job and could only stay a short time. I knew it was a lie. Before he had arrived, Janice and I both agreed Ray wouldn't be allowed to smoke in the apartment. Ma was on oxygen. Alison wasn't even crawling. When I told him, he got a little pissed off.

He didn't say it, but I knew he was leaving after two days because we made him go outside and smoke on the balcony.

On Christmas afternoon, he announced he was heading out. The turkey was in the oven. The table wasn't even set. On the drive to the bus terminal, I tried to convince him to stay, telling him Ma wasn't doing so good.

"Listen Ray, she's going down fast."

On the platform, the bus idling beside us, I pleaded with him, "Stay a few more days."

Crushing a cigarette under the toe of his boot, he picked up his duffle bag, put it over his shoulder and started up the steps into the bus. He turned and grinned "Can't. I got to go. See ya Mike. Say *bye* to everyone."

A week into the New Year, Ma was dead and I had no way to contact Ray. He missed the funeral. I had her buried next to our father.

Ma, Ray, Donny and I, that part of my life is over. My family is Janice, the girls. Where I can, I fit Donny in. I miss Ray. I miss Ma. For me, her dying was a big deal. After it happened I tried telling Janice about things. It wasn't easy, I didn't tell her much.

I remove the towel from Donny's shoulders. Shake the hair off. Fold it and put it away. I place the scissors in the drawer and then sweep the rest of the hair into a pile. When it's all swept up, I put the dustpan and the broom back where they go.

I pat Donny on the shoulder. "Got to go, Don, Janice'll have dinner almost ready."

He gets up slowly, slides the stool under the counter, walks me to the stairs. I pick up my black leather bag I've left by the door. We stare at each other. I invite him over to the house.

"Why don't you come and have supper with us? It's not far, just the other side of Coxwell," I remind him.

Looking around the room, he shakes his head, scratches his neck, "Yeah. Sure. Sometime."

As I'm saying goodbye, I notice a length of hair I've missed. It's uneven. I want to fix it. Dropping the bag to the floor, I go for the stool, telling Donny to sit back down a second.

Taking my arm, he stops me. With his other hand, his picks up the bag, raising it out toward me. "No. Go home. Your family's waiting. We'll get it next time."

I don't speak. I take the bag. I leave.

BEER BOTTLES
AND BOWLING BALLS

Gordon sniffs model glue. Sometimes when Ray and me go by his place, he'll come to the side door with glue and a plastic bag stuck around his nose and mouth. When he's high on glue, he can barely open his eyes. Once, when he was sniffing, he lit his face on fire trying to light a cigarette. Now his cheeks look like the wrinkly skin of a balloon after most of the air has seeped out.

Gordon's a friend of Ray's. They've been friends since grade school. Ray's telling him all the time to stop with the glue. Ray's always stuck up for Gordon. A lot of guys like to punch Gordon's head in. I'm not sure why. Gordon doesn't do anything to anybody. Most of the time if Ray's there he can talk them out of it. Not all the time, though. If it wasn't for Ray, I think Gordon would never leave his basement. When he isn't at school, or at the walk-in clinic getting his head sewn up, he's in his basement making model airplanes, or sniffing glue and listening to music with his headphones on.

When he was a kid, Gordon's dad did stuff to him. Around the time Gordon burnt his face, his sister Missy disappeared. She was in a few of my classes. I liked her. The police looked for her for a while. I don't think Missy was her real name.

The rain had stopped by the time we pulled out of the lane behind our house. The radio was playing country music. While Ray was messing around with the radio trying to get something else, he told Donny to stop at Gordon's. He said we had time because none of the guys would be down in the valley until after nine.

Donny said no. "Why do you want that fuckin' idiot to come? There's gonna be too many guys there who'll kick his head in. Anyway, there ain't no room for him."

Donny had come home with a brown Chevette. Even though it was a four-door, it was real small. Donny and Ray put me in the back seat and then piled firewood and the beer all around me. We needed dry wood for the fire, so Donny and Ray yanked a bunch of boards off the Chinaman's fence who lives behind us. They busted them in two and then shoved them in all around me. It was sort of funny, I couldn't hardly move when they were done. The Chevette was so full, the hatch wouldn't close. It had to be tied down with rope.

As we were driving along the Danforth, the exhaust fumes were coming up into the back of the car and going to my head.

No matter which way he turned the dial, all Ray could get was the same country station. He told Donny again to stop at Gordon's. Donny didn't answer. The needle on the radio jerked back and forth as Ray twisted the dial.

Ray said Gordon could squeeze in the back. Turning, Ray nodded at me, "Right, Mikey? He'll fit back there."

A piece of wood was pressing into my ribs. I couldn't move my legs. There was shit or mould smeared on the board I was resting my arm on. "I guess."

We stopped at a red light. Donny found me in the rearview mirror, "*Right, Mikey*," he mimicked Ray, "maybe Buttfuck could sit on your lap. *Right, Mikey? I guess.* What are you, fuckin' fag or something?" He stared at me in the rearview mirror.

Buttfuck is what Donny calls Gordon sometimes, because that's what Donny said his dad did to him.

When Donny calls Gordon Buttfuck, Ray gets pissed off. Yanking the small chrome dial off the radio, Ray threw it at Donny, telling him, "Shut the fuck up and go by his place. We'll get him in. He can lay in the back on the wood."

When we got to Gordon's, it was raining. Donny said we ain't waiting. Moving a case of beer off his feet, Ray got out of the car and hurried up the driveway, his shoulders hunched, to the side door. After knocking a couple of times, the screen door opened and Ray went inside.

The DJ on the radio said something about a Hank Williams song. I felt like I was going to puke. I moved a few boards and rolled down the window. The rain wet my face. Donny asked if I had any smokes. I said I did. Some were in my jacket pocket but there were too many boards around me to get one out. I asked Donny to turn the car off for a minute. He said he could not.

The rain stopped. Ray's been in Gordon's for about five or ten minutes. Even though there are no boards or cases of beer crowding Donny, he was too tall to fit behind the steering wheel. From the backseat, Donny looked like a crippled spider, his knees bent toward his chest and his long arms folded at the elbows.

"We're leaving," he said, reaching for the shifter.

"Wait. I'll go see what's taking them so long."

There was a sour taste in my mouth. Donny got out of the car and came around to my side to help me get out.

"Tell 'em we're leaving," he said, picking up the splinters of wood that had fallen onto the sidewalk.

Stretching, I put my jacket on. I spit and then hurried up the driveway, the warm spring air made me feel normal again.

I opened the screen door, but before I could knock, Donny called me back to the car. He was smiling. Pointing at my jacket pocket, he said, "Gimme a smoke."

Mrs. Daniels answered the door wearing tight black polyester pants and a bright green blouse. Her stomach bulged over the elastic waistband. She smiled and told me to come in. Her hair is blond at the ends, but near her scalp it's black and oily. It's piled up on her head, held off her face with a plastic gold hair clip.

The Daniels' house smelled like their dog. It smelled like other things too. Like dirty laundry and burnt food. There are boots and shoes all over the stairs. The walls are scuffed with black marks and halfway down the stairs, someone punched their fist through the wall. Behind the door, near the floor, the wall's bashed in.

The Daniels are on welfare. When Donny calls Gordon a welfare case, Ray tells him he doesn't know what he's talking about, that the Daniels aren't on welfare, they actually get a disability cheque because Mr. Daniels can't work.

When I ask Mrs. Daniels where Ray and Gordon are, she ignores me and keeps talking. She's always saying how polite Ray and me are. The problem with being polite to Mrs. Daniels is, she never stops talking. Standing on the small landing at the top of the basement stairs, she asks about Ma. I just nod and she keeps talking. She never asks about Donny. From the basement, I hear Gordon telling Ray about a model airplane he's doing. Outside, Donny's laying on the horn. Mrs. Daniels pretends she doesn't hear it.

While she keeps talking, I look into Mrs. Daniels' face, at the pink puffy flesh below her eyes. I look for something about her that reminds me of Missy. There's nothing.

When Mrs. Daniels leaned against the railing, I could see past her into their kitchen. Mr. Daniels was sitting at the table drinking something through a straw. His cane was hooked on the back of the vinyl chair beside him. Curled under the table was their wiener dog, Doreen. Once, Ray tried to convince Donny and me that Doreen was a seeing-eye dog.

"Who the fuck has a seeing-eyed wiener dog?" Donny laughed. I don't think Mr. Daniels is really even blind.

Mr. Daniels was normal until Ronny Rusk's dad beat the shit out of him. When I was ten we used to go to the community centre and play floor hockey and dodge ball in the gym. That summer, Mr. Daniels started The Boys' Boxing Club of East York. There wasn't a real ring, but Mr. Daniels got some yellow rope and four orange pylons and spaced them out to make a square. He rammed four floor hockey sticks into the holes in the tops of the pylons and then looped the rope around each stick. Mr. Daniels had a few pairs of red leather boxing gloves, but we weren't allowed to use them. We all had to share a pair of gloves and the same rubbery mouth guard. At the end of the summer, he promised we'd all get T-shirts.

For fifty cents, boys would take turns getting into the ring with Mr. Daniels. He told us he grew up in Cabbagetown and had trained with Smilin' Pat Sullivan and Slim George. None of us knew who they were.

Before you were allowed into the ring, you had to put your two quarters into a blue velour bag. He made Gordon watch to make sure none of us ripped him off. After a couple of days, the bag would be so full of coins, it looked like the seams were going to tear open. For about ten minutes, he'd show you some moves, some footwork, how to take a punch, then Gordon would ring a bell and you'd have to give the sweaty gloves and the dripping mouth guard to the next kid who had paid his fifty cents. Ma would get angry at us because we'd always be begging her for fifty cents more so we could box again with Mr. Daniels.

Mr. Daniels was always clinching and holding the older boys. They didn't like the lessons so much. They'd rather fight. If Mr. Daniels didn't like some boy, he'd punch them in the stomach real hard. Before the boy could catch his breath, Mr. Daniels would shove him under the rope and out of the ring.

One day Ronny Rusk's dad came by the community centre. Boxing was over for the day. We were playing floor hockey. Mr. Daniels was in a bathroom stall making Ronny give him a hand job. Mr. Rusk smashed Mr. Daniels' face into the sink and dragged him out of the bathroom and hit him on the head with a floor hockey stick until it broke. Then he made him set up the ring again. Mr. Daniels' face was covered in blood.

Mr. Rusk told us we had to watch and then he pounded Mr. Daniels' head in. Every time he'd fall down, Mr. Rusk would kick him in the chest and then make him get back up. I remember Ray telling Gordon he shouldn't look, but Gordon said he wanted to. While Mr. Rusk and Mr. Daniels were in the ring, Donny guarded the door. When Mr. Rusk got tired, he took off his gloves and used the bag of quarters on Mr. Daniels' head.

About a week later, I was in net and found one of Mr. Daniels' teeth. When I showed Ray, he made me give it to Gordon so he could give it back to his dad.

Mrs. Daniels was still talking when Gordon and Ray finally came upstairs. Gordon was carrying a blue and red Adidas gym bag filled with camping gear. He had a frayed yellow rope looped over his shoulder. Ray was behind him carrying a sleeping bag.

In the driveway, Gordon said, "Hey, Mikey." He handed me the rope. "We can make a Tarzan swing," he said.

I told him it was a bush party, not a camp out. Gordon smiled at me. He was always smiling and he always looked like he was about to cry, both at the same time.

The only things Donny let Gordon put in the car was a flashlight, the rope and three cans of Campbell's soup that were in the Adidas bag. Donny threw the sleeping bag and the rest of Gordon's stuff onto the wet brown grass at the front of Gordon's house, and then Donny and Ray fitted Gordon into the back of the Chevette. He was lying on top of the boards on his stomach, his arms and legs spread like he was falling. His back nearly touched the roof of the car. After they got Gordon in, Donny and Ray got me in. As we pulled away from the sidewalk, I looked into Gordon's scarred face and he smiled at me. He said, "Hey, Mikey" like he just noticed I was there.

We drove along Donlands to Overlea Boulevard, streetlights racing past, their yellow-orange glow reflected in puddles of rainwater. Every time we hit a red light, Donny would stop too fast and Gordon would slide forward on the pile of busted fence boards. He'd smash his face into the back of the headrest, and we'd laugh. Just before the light turned green, Donny would gun it and Gordon would slide backward, the bottom of his boots bashing into the tied-down hatch.

Stepping hard on the accelerator, the Chevette jerked forward. Donny yelled into the rearview mirror, "You alright back there, Buttfuck?" Gordon didn't hear him, though. He had tried to turn sideways thinking he wouldn't be tossed around as much. Instead, he ended up wedged at the very back of the car.

At first, it was funny, but I was glad when Ray told Donny to stop it. The jerking back and forth and the exhaust fumes were making me feel sick again. We passed the mall and as we were crossing the Woolco Bridge, I could see down into the valley. It was still too early for the trees to have any leaves. The branches looked like black jagged bones, snapped abruptly and piercing the dark. I wondered if any of the guys were down there already. Pressing my forehead against the chilled window, I searched for the warm glow of a bonfire but saw nothing.

Don Mills Road curved down into the valley. Before following it to the bottom, Donny said he was going to stop a second at the 7-Eleven to get a pack of smokes.

Donny parked under the Woolco Bridge. Woolco closed and left the mall a long time ago but we still call it the Woolco Bridge. People who live on the other side call it something else.

Ray helped me out of the car. As I'm stretching, I look up at the underside of the bridge. It was about a hundred feet to the top. There are thick, H-shaped concrete pillars reaching up from the ground. Running from one end to the other are four rows of ribbed yellow steel beams. It was too dark to see the catwalk. Before they blocked it off, we used to climb out on it and drop stuff off like beer bottles and bowling balls. About two years ago, Jimmy Buso got high and fell and broke his arm and both his legs. That's when they put the gate up.

From where I stood below the bridge, it was impossible to see the cars and buses going by overhead. The whine from the wet road beneath their tires gave away their passing. Runoff poured through drain pipes under the bridge. By the time this second rain reached the valley floor, it had changed into a grey soiled mist.

Like tall candles, the streetlights along the side of the bridge towered high above the valley, casting yellow cones of light down upon the roadway. Their light was too weak to reach us down here.

We unloaded the fence boards and the beer and Gordon.

Some of the guys came over and helped, then we followed them along a slippery path, up a slope and into the bush. The earth was soft from the rain. My shoes were soaked. It was dark and wet and hard to see. I was behind Gordon, carrying his rope and some boards. Gordon tripped. I stopped and the guys behind me bumped into one another. Gordon got up, and then he tripped again. He was soaked and his clothes were muddy.

"Where's your flashlight, Gordie?" I said, trying to help him.

"Oh yeah." The flashlight came on. He started walking backwards. "Hey, Mikey, check this out." He put the flashlight under his chin, the light shining over his face. His head resembled a giant white jack-o'-lantern with hollow eyes and slashed cheeks.

Up ahead, someone howled and a guy named Riley went *who who who* like an owl. Gordon tripped again. He dropped the flashlight. Behind me, a guy named Steve asked Donny why the fuck we brought him.

They had a fire going, but it was small. In a few minutes Donny got it going good. Some of the guys dragged a couple of picnic benches closer to the fire. Gordon stumbled around in the dark. He lost the flashlight again.

Most of the guys were friends of Donny's and Ray's. I recognized Mitchell and Travis and a guy named Hank. He's Chinese, but he's okay. His parents own a Vietnamese grocery store. Crouching by the fire, Hank was using a jackknife to tear strips of bark from a wet branch, the polished blade gleaming in the fire light.

We sat around the fire drinking beer and smoking. Every so often, everyone was quiet and we just listened to the crackling as the fence boards burned. Hank pulled out a bag of weed. Ray and him rolled a couple of joints and we passed them around. Gordon took off his jacket and jeans and hung them on sticks close to the fire to dry. He sat on a log in a pair of dirty long johns, his skinny legs too near the fire. His boots were caked with mud and tied too tight. We all laughed at the shirt he was wearing. It was purple and white and long sleeved with a drawing of *Prince* on the front and the words *When Doves Cry* on the back. He tried to pretend to laugh, but he was shivering too much. Ray gave Gordon his jacket. Gordon stared into the fire, looking at the flames like they were telling him a secret.

The fire was warm. We were loud, telling stories and lies and laughing at stuff that wasn't even funny. Donny tossed the three cans of Campbell's soup into the fire. Orange flames, working like fingers, unwrapped the red labels, burning them. A few minutes later, there was a muffled *pop*, and then another muffled *pop* as the cans ruptured. Gordon was sprayed with chicken bits and noodles and corn.

Getting up, he wiped his face on the sleeve of Ray's jacket. He took it off and gave it back to Ray. Even though his wasn't dry, he put it on anyway. He left his jeans hanging on the stick to keep drying.

Picking up his rope, he looked at me and asked, "Anyone wanna make a Tarzan swing?" No one answered, not even Ray. After he disappeared beyond the circle of firelight, Travis kicked over the stick that Gordon's jeans were drying on. They fell into the fire. Before they burned too much, Ray got them out.

Donny put more wood onto the fire. Hank showed us a trick with his jackknife. He passed it quickly back and forth from one hand to the other. He balanced the point of the blade on his flat palm. A tiny pool of blood appeared. Before he could finish the trick, Gordon came running up the trail, yelling "Holy fuck holy fuck" over and over again.

He nearly ran into the fire. The jackknife fell. Hank put his hand to his mouth, tasting his blood.

"What'd ya see, Buttfuck? Something scare ya?" Donny chuckled.

He couldn't say anything else but, "Holy fuck holy fuck." He was trembling, too.

Donny said to Ray, "Hey Ray, something's wrong with your girlfriend."

"Holy fuck holy fuck. I fell right on her."

Ray got up slowly. He went over to Gordon.

"Fell on who, Gordie?" Ray put his hand on Gordon's shoulder. He leaned in close to Gordon's scarred face "Fell on who?" he asked once more.

Gordon started back with the "holy fuck" again.

Donny shoved Gordon hard. As Gordon fell backward, Donny's fingers snapped closed into tight fists. "What the fuck is wrong with you?"

Covering his face, Gordon lay on the wet ground on his back. "I fell right on her."

Donny stood over him. "Fell on who, Buttfuck?"

"The lady under the bridge."

We all looked at each other for a second, and then took off toward the bridge to see what Gordon was talking about.

There was a lady on the ground on her side below the bridge. She wasn't too far from the Chevette. Gordon's rope was coiled on top of her. She looked as though she was sleeping, but one of her legs was twisted the wrong way. None of us got too close.

"She's a Paki," Travis whispered as though he might wake her.

"Maybe someone dumped her here," Mitchell whispered.

Donny looked up at the bridge. "Jumped," he announced. "Look at her leg."

They did. Then they all took off, except for Donny and Ray and me.

Donny knelt beside her. Ray and me moved closer. I could hear Gordon. He was running toward us in his long johns with the flashlight on.

When he shone it on the lady, he started again with the "holy fuck."

Ray pointed at the lady's face, "Shine it there," he told Gordon. He did but the light was unsteady.

When she hit the ground, her face must have hit a rock because her teeth were broke and some came out of her mouth. They reminded me of busted pieces of corn. Her eyes were open. They looked afraid.

Something moved under the lady's coat. Even Donny was startled. Gordon was out of his mind. Donny went over to him, grabbed him by the collar and punched him once in the face. There was a loud cracking sound. Gordon dropped to the ground.

Ray said, "Donny, let's get outta here." I could tell Ray was scared. So was I.

Something moved again under the lady's coat. Ray picked up Gordon's flashlight and shined it on her stomach. She had jumped holding something in her arms.

"Let's get out of here, Mikey. Come on, Donny. Let's go."

Donny told Ray to hold the flashlight steady. He undid the top two buttons on her coat and gently lifted the lady's limp arm. He rested it on her side. The other one flopped into the soft earth, the fingers opening slowly like flower petals. Her palm was covered with orange lines that looked like words in another language. Donny undid the rest of the buttons and opened the coat.

It was a baby. It was alive but there was blood coming out of its ears.

"Donny. Donny. Let's go. Leave it. Let's go." Ray was frightened.

Donny picked up the baby. It made a noise. It kicked its legs a little.

"Gimme your jacket," he said to me.

I didn't move. He told me again to take off my jacket. I could not move. My mouth was open. I stared at the lady. Her braided hair was so long. It had become tangled in the coil of rope Gordon dropped on her.

"Gimme your fuckin' jacket, Mikey."

As I took it off, Ray said, "Leave it. Put it back. Let's get out of here."

"We can't just leave it. It's a fuckin' baby." Donny wrapped my jacket around the baby. He held it against his chest. "We'll take it up to the 7-Eleven. The guy who's working there's a Paki." Looking down at the baby, its tiny head cupped in his huge hand, he said, "It's one of theirs."

Donny started toward the path that led out of the valley. I hurried behind him.

Ray yelled, "What about Gordie?"

Donny yelled back, "Fuck'im."

Except for a taxi and a parked car, the parking lot was empty. We stayed at the side of the store where there was hardly any light. I could smell the garbage from the bins. It started to rain.

None of us looked at the baby. It was moving under my jacket.

"What if it starts cryin'?" I ask, but Donny doesn't answer. He told me to go to the corner and make sure no one was coming. He told Ray to go find a box or something to put the baby in. Ray went around to the back of the store and then came back with a plastic bag.

"Here," he said, handing it to Donny, "Come on, just let's go."

"You can't put a baby in a fuckin' plastic bag." Donny pulled the bag from Ray's hand.

Ray went back behind the store. This time he came back with a plastic shopping basket. The handle was busted off. Donny put the baby into it, covering it with my jacket.

"My jacket!"

"It's gotta stay warm."

"Let's just get out of here."

Ray passed the basket to me.

"I don't want it," I told them.

"The guy'll remember me." Donny said, "He knows what I look like."

"They got cameras, Mikey," Ray added nervously.

The sweatshirt I was wearing had a hood. Ray pulled it up. It covered my face.

"When you get in there, just don't look up."

No one was at the cash register as I pulled open the door. A buzzer sounded. I kept my head down. There was a pounding in my ears. I looked down at the basket. The baby whimpered.

I set the basket on the counter.

I didn't look up until we were running across Don Mills Road in the pouring rain.

The next afternoon Ray came into the bedroom and woke me up. It was Sunday. Ma was at work. He held up a newspaper. I was on the front of *The Sun*. Sitting up in bed, I looked at the front page. It showed me putting the basket on the counter. They got the picture from the security camera. It wasn't so clear and you couldn't see my face.

I followed Ray into the kitchen in my underwear. "Hey Donny, check this out, Mikey's famous." Donny was eating Cheez Whiz out of the jar with a fork.

I couldn't stop thinking about the baby or about the lady's teeth. Donny and Ray acted like everything was normal. They told me not to mention anything to Ma. I went back into the bedroom and got dressed.

Ray sat at the kitchen table eating Shreddies from the box. With his mouth filled with cereal, he read the headline to Donny and me, "*Big Gulp Baby*. Shit. What kinda stupid headline is that?"

He put another handful of Shreddies into his mouth. In smaller letters below the picture he read, "*Mystery Baby Abandoned at 7-Eleven*." He read the article out loud. They interviewed the store manager. It didn't say anything about the lady.

The next day around supper time, the police came to the house. Ray answered the door. Donny told me to go into the bedroom. With the bedroom door opened a little, I could see one of the officers.

They wanted to step in but Donny wouldn't let them. They wanted to talk about the lady and Gordon and the Chevette.

"No one's in trouble," the officer said, "She left a note. We just want to talk to whoever's involved."

"Involved?" Ray asked. He told them we weren't even there.

I heard the other officer say something about Gordon Daniels.

"Who?" Ray asked.

They went on like this for a while. The officers were getting frustrated. "Listen," one of them said, "honestly, I don't give a shit about some disturbed woman who took a header off a bridge. We just wanna finish up the paperwork and move on. But we can't until we talk with your brother." He reached into his vest. "Here," he handed Donny a card. "Tell Mike to call me, or come by the station. Whatever he wants. He isn't in trouble. We just gotta close this thing up. Okay?"

After a few days there was nothing else in the paper. I could not get it out of my head, though. I even thought about going by Gordon's. I figured he'd be high, so I didn't.

On my way home from school a police car pulled up beside me. It was the same officers that had come by the house. They told me to get in. I told them I didn't want to.

"However you want it, Mike."

With the cruiser idling, I rested my arms on the door and leaned in the window. One of the officers asked all the questions. The other one wrote everything down in a small black book with a black pen. I told them about the baby. I told them Donny and Ray and me were walking behind the valley when we found the lady under the bridge.

"What about Gordon Daniels?"

"Oh yeah, he was there, too."

They didn't ask about the Chevette. The radio crackled. They ignored it. It crackled a second time and the officer who was writing everything down picked up a telephone from between the seats on the console and started talking.

They had to go. They thanked me for cooperating.

"If there's anything else, give us a call." He handed me a card. He told me not to worry about anything.

Before I could ask about the baby, the tires squealed and the cruiser pulled away.

Whenever I mentioned the lady or the baby to Donny and Ray, they'd get pissed off. When they went out, I stayed home with Ma.

Ma asked if I was okay.

"Yeah."

The first time I telephoned Officer Rideout, it was his day off. They told me to leave my number and he'd call me back. I could not. I was calling from a phone booth. When I finally got through to him, I had to remind him who I was.

I didn't know why I was calling. I didn't have anything else to tell him. Twisting the phone cord around my finger, I closed my eyes and could see the lady's hair, the braid tangled in Gordon's rope.

"What—" I swallowed, "what happened to the baby?"

Officer Rideout said, "I'm not sure."

"Well, umm, could you tell me—" Chewing the corner of my thumbnail, I remembered the lady's hand, her fingers opening so slowly. "Could you tell me where the baby is now? So I could find out?"

"I'm not permitted to divulge that information."

"Oh, okay. Thanks." I hung up.

Ma gave me an envelope a few days later. It was in the mailbox. My name was typed on the front. Inside, on a piece of paper was an address. It was typed. Written below in black ink and circled were the words, *the father*.

"What is it?" Ma asked.

"Nothing."

The apartment building was close to the Woolco Bridge. The lock on the door in the lobby was broken. The intercom didn't work. I got on the elevator with an old man who had a thick black beard. He was wearing sandals and clothes that looked like pajamas. He was pulling a bundle buggy filled with folded bed sheets and towels and an orange box of Tide.

The doors closed slowly. The elevator smelled like piss. The plastic buttons you press for your floor had been burnt with a lighter. Some of them were melted.

The hallway smelled like other people's food. Reaching into my pocket, I took out the piece of paper with the typed address and unfolded it. From behind an apartment door came the sound of a child crying. From another, a TV blared. Slowly, I walked down the hall, studying the numbers on each door, my shoes brushing against the flattened soiled carpet.

His apartment was at the end of the hallway, next to the stairwell. I stood in front of the apartment door. There was no sound coming from inside. A brilliant beam of sunlight shone through the peephole.

I thought about leaving, about going home, but somehow, the bright ray of light bursting through from the peephole held me there.

I knocked. The peephole went dark. The woman who opened the door had an earring in her nose. She asked if she could help me.

"I—" The inside of my mouth went dry. "I'm looking for—"

Holding up the paper, I said softly, "I found the baby."

"Oh." She lowered her head and told me to come in. She wasn't wearing anything on her feet.

"Please. Sit." The apartment was clean and there wasn't much furniture, just a lamp on a coffee table and a couch that sat low to the floor. There were green pillows with gold tassels scattered on the parquet floor. A large blue carpet with the sun and the moon and stars sewn into it hung on the wall behind the couch. The walls were painted white. Too much sunlight came into the living room. There was a red baby rattle on the windowsill. They had no curtains. The glare hurt my eyes.

I sat on the low couch. Two women spoke quietly in the kitchen. One of them came and asked if I'd like a tea.

"No thank you."

A man came into the living room. I stood and we shook hands. He was wearing the same type of clothes as the old man on the elevator, but his beard wasn't as thick. He was only a couple of years older then Donny.

"My name is Aly. Please," he sat down on the couch, "sit." Neither of us spoke. Leaning forward, I rubbed my hands together, listening to the women in the kitchen. Their voices were so quiet, as though they were breathing out their words, not speaking them.

A toilet flushed in another apartment. When I spoke, my voice sounded too loud in the nearly empty living room. "I wanted to find out what—" I couldn't continue.

Aly leaned forward, resting his elbows on his knees. He pressed the tips of his fingers together. As I began to speak again, he turned but looked past me, into the blinding glare of the sunlight. The whites of his eyes were snaked with red veins.

"What happened to—" One of women came into the living room carrying a bowl of pistachio nuts and a bowl of sunflower seeds. Aly waved her away before she could offer them.

"What happened to the ba—?"

Aly said, "My wife, Zahra, she said, she is happy here. She said, she love this new life in Canada."

I tried again, "What—"

"Everything will be good here, Zahra tells me. I believe her."

We were both quiet. I thought the women in the kitchen were listening. I wished I hadn't come here. "Maybe she was upset about something," I said.

"Upset?"

"When she, you know, when she went to the bridge." I should have done what Donny and Ray did and just forgot about the whole thing.

"What she did is unforgivable. The Prophet, peace be upon him, says, 'whoever purposely throws himself from a mountain and kills himself will be in Fire falling down into it forever.' Forever."

I didn't know what to say, so I asked about the baby again.

"She is fine. She is with her auntie now."

We sat in silence. From the apartment above came a thumping sound as though someone was bouncing a ball.

I didn't know how to leave. One of the women in the kitchen offered me tea again. Aly would start to tell me something about himself and his wife, but then his words would trail off until only his lips were moving.

"I have to go now." I stood up. Aly didn't move.

Looking up at me he said, "I am sorry you found her like that. It is terrible the way she was. I know, I washed her body. I know how broken it was. It was terrible. Terrible."

He covered his face in his hands. "It was terrible what you saw beneath the bridge, yes, but it is more terrible now. For me, when I close my eyes, I see her. I see her always falling."

I left Aly in the apartment, crying on the couch. At the elevator, I held my finger on the down button to make it come faster. Aly came out of his apartment. I jabbed at the button. He raised his hand, telling me to wait. He came to me and put his arms around my shoulders. His beard was rough against my face. He smelled like sweat and food.

He wept. "Thank you for not leaving my baby alone," he whispered. I put my hand on Aly's back. The elevator doors opened. The old man in the sandals stood there looking at us, the bundle buggy empty, except for the orange box of Tide.

RADIO DISPATCHED

I don't remember any of this. I was too young when it all happened. Ray told me the whole story one afternoon when I came home from work early. Just me and him were in the house. We were in the kitchen at the table eating Frosted Flakes without milk. Ma was at work and Donny was out somewhere. Ray got up from the table and went down to the basement. I heard stuff like paint cans and mason jars being moved around. When he came back up, he sat down and then slid a folded piece of newspaper across the table.

When I picked it up, he said, "Careful. It'll fall apart."
The paper had turned yellow, like tea had been spilled on it. It smelled like the basement. As I was unfolding it, some of the creases tore. To keep it together, I laid it on the table.

It was an article cut out of a newspaper called *The Toronto Telegram*. I never heard of that paper before. Across the top it said, *Bad Accident Kills Good Samaritan on DVP*. In smaller letters below that it said, *Father lured to his death by disobedient son*. As I was reading this, Ray put a spoonful of dry cereal into his mouth and said, "Don't say anything to Ma. She doesn't know I saved it." I nodded. "And whatever you do Mikey, don't mention it to Donny."

There was a photograph. A lot of it was covered with mould. It showed a police officer directing cars around something lying on the highway. Drivers had slowed to look. Traffic was backed up, snaking around the thing which had been covered with a plastic tarp. The officer's arm was raised, waving at the drivers to get a move on. He looked pissed off because they won't keep moving. On the shoulder of the highway there was a police car and a tow truck, and in the distance, a fire truck was blocking another lane. Written on the boom of the tow truck were the words, RADIO DISPATCHED.

Ray came around to my side of the table. Leaning over my shoulder, he put his finger on the photograph. "See that tow truck. It was ours. An old Ford Super Duty." Ray moved his finger from the tow truck to the back window of the police car. "And see that?" he said, "That's where I'm sitting, but you can't see me 'cause I'm too little, but you can just make out the top of Donny's head, right there—"

Ray kept talking but I wasn't listening anymore. I read the caption below the photograph. It said that the thing on the highway that everyone was slowing to take a look at was our father. We never talk about him. Before this, I had never seen a photograph of him, either.

Ray said that once we were like a normal family. We used to do things like normal people did. Like have our own house and go to a cottage. We used to live in a big house on Fairview Avenue in Riverdale. One of our favourite places to go to was the Riverdale Zoo, because it was close and because it was free. We could walk there. Ma would push me in a carriage. We'd walk out to Broadview, down the hill and across the Riverdale flats. They built a pedestrian bridge over the Don Valley Parkway. Ray and Donny were always getting in trouble for spitting on cars as they passed under the bridge.

Now the Riverdale Zoo is a farm. They don't have monkeys and other zoo animals there anymore. Ray said we went there a lot on weekends. In the winter, when the zoo was closed, we'd go tobogganing down the hills at Riverdale Park. I don't remember any of that.

Our father was a mechanic at Robinson's Chevrolet on the Danforth, near Coxwell. It's gone now. Sometimes, they'd let him drive home new cars. He drove a tow truck, too. There was a garage at the back of the house on Fairview. He had all sorts of tools and equipment in there like compressors and cutting torches. To make a little extra money, he would tow cars home and work on them. When he'd be working on a car, Donny and Ray were allowed to help. I wasn't. Ma told him not to take me out to the garage. She said at three, I was too little.

"Sometimes," Ray told me, "when Ma wasn't around, Dad would get a small plastic lawn chair or a paint can and set it off to one side so you could watch us. He'd tell you not to move. You never did."

One time when him and Ray and Donny were underneath a car, Ma came out and saw me sitting on the lawn chair and got upset. She asked our father how he was supposed to keep an eye on me if he was underneath a car. She said it wasn't safe and that I was too young and what if something caught on fire? Ray said he did not know what the big deal was because all I'd ever do was sit there watching them or look around at all the stuff in the garage. Ma picked me up and carried me back into the house anyway.

If there were no cars to work on, Donny and Ray were allowed to play in the tow truck. They knew how to work the boom. They'd take turns making it go up and down. Our father showed them how to work the CB radio. He told them they could play with it, so long as they never actually switched it on.

Ray said him and Donny would pretend they were tow truck operators. One of them would be the driver and one of them would be dispatch. Ray would crouch on the steel running board outside the tow truck on the passenger side. He'd have a walkie-talkie. He was dispatch. He'd radio Donny telling him there was a lady who needed help with a flat tire, or about a man locked out of his car. They'd talk back and forth through the rolled-down window, beginning each sentence with, "Ten-four, big buddy." That's what they called the game, Ten-Four, Big Buddy.

When the pretend dispatch was over, Ray would climb in through the window and they'd pretend to drive to where the person needed help.

One day when they were playing, our father came into the garage. "He must have been standing outside listening to us," Ray said, "because he told us that he did more than change tires and use a slim jim." He told them both to get into the truck. Crouching beside the rolled-down window with the walkie-talkie, he pretended to be dispatch. He radioed that a car was flipped onto its side on Broadview, then he got in the tow truck and Donny pretended to drive them there. On the way, he told them there'd be fluids spilled on the road, like gasoline and motor oil, so they'd have to put sand down.

"We'll probably need the bumper winch for this one," he added. When they got to the pretend car accident, he told Donny and Ray other things to do.

When someone traded in a wreck at the dealership, it was our father's job to haul it to the auto wreckers out in Cookstown. If he needed parts for a car he was working on, he'd go to a scrapyard down around Cherry Beach. When he'd go on a Saturday, he'd take Donny and Ray. Ma never let me go with them.

Our father was friends with the men who worked at the yard. A lot of them were Guyanese. Some of them lived in the sheds beside the office. Ray said when they talked, they were hard to understand. There was a big dog there too, but nobody was afraid of it anymore.

When he'd be done dropping the car he'd brought in, or when he was done getting the parts he needed, our father would go into the office and sit down and talk with the workers about cars and other stuff. Even though kids weren't supposed to be in the yard, Donny and Ray were allowed. The man who ran the place told them not to climb up on anything. He told them to stay clear of the crusher and the shredder.

The oldest cars were piled at the back of the yard. That's where Donny and Ray would go to look for hood ornaments and hub-caps. Ray said that there were a lot of cars way in the back that nobody needed parts for anymore. Cars like Buick Sedanettes, Cranbrooks and Cords.

I'd never heard of those kinds of cars before.

They'd stay back there collecting stuff until they'd hear the tow truck start up. They were allowed take one hubcap and one hood ornament each.

Back home in the garage, they'd clean the hubcaps and polish them. Once they were shiny, our father would hammer nails into the two-by-four studs and hang them up. Donny cut a board with a handsaw and our father let Ray drill holes through it so they could mount the hood ornaments. Some of them were so big, they had to be mounted on their own piece of wood.

Ray told me he remembers one from a '48 or '49 Packard. "It was a flying lady, or an angel or maybe a swan," he said "All chrome, and so fuckin' huge, I remember imagining that if it ever came alive, it would tear off the front end of the car and carry it to heaven."

Everything was normal until the accident in the newspaper happened. They were going up the Don Valley Parkway hauling a wreck to Cookstown. Even though it was a Saturday, there was a lot of traffic. Somewhere around the Eglinton on ramp, they passed a car stopped on the shoulder. Ray said he never remembered passing it, but when they got to up to Lawrence Avenue and our father headed for the off ramp, Ray asked why they were leaving the highway.

"Didn't you see that car on the shoulder back there? She's got a flat."

Donny said, "You told us you did more than just help people change flat tires. Let someone else help 'er. "

"But it's a lady, Donald. And there was a baby beside her on the seat. We can't just leave her and the baby."

On Lawrence they made a quick U-turn and started back toward the ramp in the other direction. "Don't worry, boys, this won't take long."

It took a few minutes to double back. Ray said when they got there, the lady had her head against the steering wheel. When they pulled up in front of her, she looked up. Ray could tell she was crying. The car did have a flat. There was a baby in the front seat, too.

Cars passed. A transport truck went by. It was so close, the tow truck rocked. Our father looked in the side-view mirror waiting for a break in the traffic so he could open his door. While he was watching the oncoming traffic in the mirror, he told Donny and Ray to sit tight. "I'm going to go change 'er flat. Then we'll be on our way."

"Can we help?" Donny asked.

Our father had opened the door a little but then closed it hard. Turning to face them, he said, "Don't either one of you get out of the truck. Is that clear?"

Donny and Ray just nodded.

"I remember Donny and me turning around and kneeling on the bench seat and watching him through the back window." The lady took her baby and stood back from the car while our father changed her tire. Because there was a car on the sling, Ray said it was hard to see what our father was doing. Cars and vans passed. It was noisy. Each time a truck rolled by, the tow truck rocked side to side.

"Then the lady started pointing, waving her hand to get Dad's attention. The lady was pointing across the highway. Dad finally saw her waving and stood up. He put his hands up to his head. They were looking at Donny."

Maybe it was the noise, or maybe because he was watching our father, but Ray said he never heard Donny get out of the tow truck.

"Somehow he had managed to get halfway across the highway without getting killed. He was standing near the guardrail. When the cars would let up for a second, I could see him just standing there, like nothing was the matter. He was holding a hubcap."

Our father was yelling and waving at him to get back from the highway, but it was too loud. Ray said he got scared because he could tell our father didn't know what to do. He'd run to the front of the tow truck, waving at Donny to get back, then he'd run to where the lady with the baby was and put his hands up to his head. The whole time, Donny was standing inches from the cars and trucks that went tearing by at a hundred miles an hour, holding the hubcap up to his chest like it was his shield.

Then, it happened. Right in front of Donny and Ray. Our father was at the front of the tow truck. He was still waving his arms and yelling. Ray couldn't hear him, but he could tell by the way his mouth was moving what he was saying. He was telling Donny, "Get back. Get back."

One of those delivery trucks with the sliding doors tore past. It had side-view mirrors that stuck out farther than normal. Our father was standing too close. The mirror clipped his head. Ray said he saw a piece of his face go flying. He lost his balance. He stumbled forward.

Tires squealed. "It happened so fast, I didn't know what to do," Ray said. "I was crying. People were getting out of their cars. I heard car doors slamming. People were running down the highway."

Ray said he picked up the CB radio. Even though he wasn't allowed to, he turned it on. There was static. He put the CB near his mouth and squeezed the button just like our father had taught him. The static stopped.

Up ahead, people were crouching. A man who was kneeling, stood up. Covering his mouth, he ran to the shoulder of the highway and vomited over the guardrail. The lady with the baby was screaming.

"Ten-Four, big buddy," Ray said into the CB radio. "What do we do now?" Taking his finger off the button, he waited for dispatch to reply, but all he heard was static.

The police came. There was an ambulance and fire trucks. Donny and Ray were put into the back of a police car. Ray said he was crying. He said he couldn't stop. Donny just sat there, holding the dirty hubcap to his chest. When the officer tried to take it away from him, Donny wouldn't let it go.

The officer asked them questions about what happened. Because he was crying so much, Ray couldn't talk. Donny just stared out the window.

The officer passed a packet of tissues back to Ray. Again, he asked Donny what happened. Donny wouldn't answer. Ray could tell by the way the cop was talking that he thought Donny was older than he really was. Everybody did. Donny was always big for his age.

"Son, why'd you get out of the tow truck?" When Donny did not answer, the officer turned and reached over the seat and grabbed at the hubcap. Donny held it tighter to his chest.

"You got your daddy run over for a hubcap? You're going to have to tell me what happened, son. Now, why'd you get out of the tow truck?"

Ray started to tell the officer about their collection of hubcaps and hood ornaments, but Donny told him, "Shut-up."

The officer just shook his head. He turned back and started writing something in a little black pad. Looking in the rear-view mirror, the officer asked Donny how old he was. When Donny didn't answer, Ray sniffled and told the officer that Donny was eleven.

They telephoned Ma but she wasn't at the house. The police took Donny and Ray home. They waited in the police car in the driveway for Ma. A little while later, Ma came along the sidewalk. She was pushing a stroller and carrying a grocery bag. The officer got out and then let Donny and Ray out. They went to Ma. She knew something was wrong. She dropped the bag.

Covering her mouth, she asked, "What's happened?"

The officer said they should go inside first. He'd tell her in there.

Ma screamed, "Tell me now."

When he did, Ma collapsed. Lying there on the sidewalk, she cried, "Oh please, no. Oh please, no," over and over again.

Ray told me he found out later, Ma was four months pregnant. It was supposed to be a sister. Ma lost it. I never knew about that.

After all this happened, for a while, things weren't so good. There were days when Ma wouldn't get out of bed. Donny was in charge. He told Ray to take care of me.

When the telephone would ring, Donny would say, "Don't answer it." He kept all the curtains closed. When someone knocked at the door, Ray said, "We'd all hide."

Donny told Ray not to go into the garage anymore. "Over the next few weeks, Donny gathered together everything in the house that had belonged to Dad. All his clothes, all the photographs he was in, everything, even his toothbrush and the things he'd shave with. He collected them all and took them out to the garage."

One night, Donny lit it all on fire. He poured gasoline all over the garage. The tow truck was in there. The flames reached as high as the trees in the backyard. The firemen thought something might explode. When we wouldn't come to the front door, they smashed it in and had to carry Ma out in her nightie. They went to every home on Fairview and pounded on the doors to wake everyone up. Everyone had to get out, they said, the fire might spread. It didn't.

When they got the fire out, everything was burnt.

"A few days later, Donny and you and me went out back to have a look. The police had put yellow tape around where the garage used to be. We walked through the ashes. Dad's tow truck was sitting on its rims. The plastic yellow lights that had been on the roof were melted. The paint was burnt off. The glass was gone. The body was already rusting. I picked up a hood ornament. It was covered in soot. I tried to put it in my pocket without Donny seeing but he did and told me to drop it."

While Ray was telling me about what happened after the fire, I remembered something. I remembered the smell of burnt wood. I remember stepping in ashes, ankle-deep, and kicking them up. I remembered grey clouds coming up around me. As my shoes passed through the ashes, I remembered, they made no noise.

It wasn't long before a social worker was sent to our house. They took us. Ma spent some time on the sixth floor at East General. When she was better, we lived together again. We had to move. We had to change schools. For a while, we were on welfare.

At a new school, Donny's teacher told Ma there was something wrong with him. The principal said Donny should see someone, like a counsellor or a psychologist. Ma said no way.

"We moved a few times more," Ray said. "Then Ma got the job where she's now and we've stayed here."

Ray pushed his chair from the table and got up. The box of Frosted Flakes was empty. He went to the stove and put the kettle on.

"You want a coffee?" he asked, taking the old newspaper clipping off the table in front of me and folding it up. Putting it in his shirt pocket, he told me again not to mention any of this to Donny or Ma.

The kettle whistled. He made us each a coffee. We went out on the back step and had a cigarette. Neither of us spoke. Finishing his first cigarette, Ray flicked the butt into the tall grass and then he put another between his lips. Instead of lighting it, he took the *Telegram* article from his pocket and lit it on fire. Holding it between his fingers, we watched it burn. Black bits of ash floated up above our heads.

MEET THE TEACHER

Ma can't read. When she brings forms or papers home from work that have to be filled out or read, she'll ask Ray or me to do it. She says she's too tired. Or she says her head hurts, or her eyes hurt, but I know she's just saying that. As long as I remember, whenever there was something Ma needed read, she'd rub her forehead and squint, saying just loud enough so we'd hear her, that soon, she'd need glasses.

After supper, when it's warm out, Ma sits on the back steps, soaking her feet in a basin of warm water. Sometimes she'll look through an old *Toronto Sun* she's found on the subway, or a magazine she's picked up in the lunchroom at work. She'll look at the pictures and the advertisements for a long time. If Donny and Ray go out without me and I don't feel like watching TV, I'll go out back and sit with her. She'll tell me about her shift and I'll tell her about school. A guidance counsellor told me I should think about applying to a couple of universities in the spring. I'm not sure what to do.

Every so often, I'll glance over to see what Ma's looking at in the paper. I look back and forth between the page she's on and her eyes. When she notices me doing this, she'll turn the page.

I knew Ma couldn't read since I was a kid. When I was in grade school, Ma only ever came to meet with one of my teachers, Miss Crans. That was in grade six. Ma finally went because Miss Crans wouldn't let up. All the other years, Ma would tell me to tell the teacher she couldn't get time off work. If there was important stuff they wanted her to know, she said they could tell it to Ray. He was a few grades ahead of me. He went to the same school and had some of the same teachers. Ray's marks weren't so good, but teachers liked him. When he had to, he knew how to speak like an adult.

The interviews were scheduled for the week before the Christmas break. Every year it was the same routine. Ma would tell Ray that he would have to talk with my teacher because she couldn't get the time off work.

She told him, "We need all the overtime I can get."

At first, Ray would say no, for Ma to get Donny to go. She said Donny was too busy. Back then, Donny was working at Weston's. Actually, he had two jobs, the one at Weston's and for a while another at a bakery in the mornings before school. By seventeen, he had grown a beard. The owner of the bakery told him to shave it. He wouldn't. They fired him.

Only once did Donny ever meet with my teacher. That was in grade three. The meeting was scheduled for four-thirty. Donny showed up at the house way after six driving a gold Cordoba. One window was missing and the rear seat torn out.

I was glad he was so late. We wouldn't have to go. The school would be closed. I told him it was no use, my teacher would be gone. He told me to get in the car. "We're going anyways."

We drove to the school. It was freezing and the heater wasn't working. Blasts of air burst from Donny's nose and mouth like steam from the nostrils of an angry bull. Cupping my hands in front of my mouth, I blew into them. I had no mittens. It was dark and snowing when we got to the school. As we drove through the unplowed parking lot, the back end of the Cordoba fishtailed, bald tires failing to grip the frozen asphalt.

There weren't many cars left in the lot. Then I spotted my teacher leaving through a side door. Clutching a bunch of papers and books close to her chest, she carried a huge bag slung over her shoulder. With small steps, she moved cautiously toward her car. She held car keys, ready to be slid into the lock. She was wearing a big coat, black leather gloves. Her boots were high heeled. They were leather, too.

Lowering myself into the seat, I pointed and told Donny, "That's her."

We circled around the lot, coming up behind her. The engine made a low rumbling sound. Headlights cast a yellow glare on her back. Donny nudged the car closer. She walked faster. Donny tapped the gas, jerking the car forward, nearly sliding into her.

Papers and a notebook slipped from her grasp. As they fell, she reached for them, disappearing below the hood of the car.

"Donny," I yelled, my voice cracking. A little bit more and we'd run over her. Sliding forward to the edge of the seat, I strained to see over the front. She was there, crouching, picking the notebook up from between the hard ruts of frozen snow. Standing, she continued, quicker, moving toward her car.

Donny rolled down the window. Calling out above the rumble of the engine, Donny yelled, "Hey. Hey. Hang on."

The bag slung over her shoulder slid down her arm, pulling her forward. Donny yelled again, this time punching the centre of the steering wheel. The horn didn't work.

"Fuck." He pounded harder, his knuckles white and numb.

When she turned, I could see moisture freezing on her cheeks. Pressing my face against the windshield, she recognized me.

She came around to my side of the car.

Pointing at the window, Donny ordered, "Roll it down." I couldn't. It was frozen. I tried to turn the handle with both hands. It wouldn't budge.

My teacher leaned close to the window. She looked at Donny, at me. "Are you okay, Michael?" When she spoke, plumes of frozen breath mushroomed against the window, graying the frosted glass.

Again, she asked if I was okay, her voice muffled through the window.

"Roll it down, you weak fuck," Donny snapped. Bits of ice, melting each time he exhaled, stuck to his moustache like tiny shards of vanishing glass.

Finally, the frozen seal broke and I cranked the window open.

Before she could speak, Donny leaned over and lifted me by the fake fur collar of my coat. He thrust me toward my teacher and held me there. "How's he doin'? Okay?"

My teacher didn't know what Donny was talking about. For a second, neither did I. Again, he asked, "Just tell me if he's doin' okay? In school, is he passing and shit?"

"Yes—" She looked down at me, "Michael's doing fine, but we—"

Donny cut her off. "Okay. That's all I need to know."

Shifting into drive, Donny gunned it, the rear wheels spitting chunks of black slush and ice into the empty parking lot behind us. As I rolled up the window, in the side-view mirror, I saw my teacher shivering in the parking lot, a blue-grey veil of exhaust fumes and snow flakes settling upon her.

The teacher Ma met with was Miss Crans. Miss Crans wasn't like any other teacher I ever had. She was old and spoke with an accent. She didn't know Ray. She was new. At the beginning of

December, I brought home the letter. It told Ma to check off the time and the day she could come to the school and meet with her. I showed it to Ray. Crumpling the paper into a ball, Ray told me not to worry about it.

"But Ray, she's not like other teachers."

The next day when Miss Crans asked about the letter, I told her I lost it. She sent home another one and I showed it to Ray. He did the same thing. This went on for about two weeks. By then, all the other students had handed in their letter. I kept telling Miss Crans I lost mine. Even though she was from England or some place like that, I could tell she was getting pissed off. She would take me aside at recess or after school to ask why I hadn't returned the letter. Each time she seemed a little more irritated. When she was done speaking, she'd bring her lips together, tight. They reminded me of white, bloodless leeches.

Placing a finger under my chin, she forced me to look up at her.

She took off her glasses. They hung from her neck by a silver chain. Through gritted teeth she said, "Son, you're not in any trouble." She said she was going to *ring* my mother. I told her I didn't know what that meant.

Sighing, she explained, "*Telephone* her. If this keeps up, I'll *telephone* her."

Swallowing, I wished I wasn't looking at her. I wished I could look away but she held my chin firmly as I said, "We don't have a phone."

She let my chin go. "Be truthful, Michael. You're not in any trouble. If your mother can't make it, your father will do."

Inside my damp winter boots, my toes curled. "We don't have one of those either, Miss."

She gave me another letter, the final letter, she called it, to give to Ma. This time though, Ma had to sign it. I showed the letter to Ray. He and Donny were in the living room putting up a fake Christmas tree. Ma wasn't home. She was working a double. Ray was trying to figure out the lights. None of them worked. Donny was forcing the fake branches into holes in the green wooden pole which was screwed to a stand. He couldn't get a lot of the branches to fit into the holes. Ornaments, blue and red, smeared with fake snow, were scattered all over the carpet. The fake angel that went on top of the tree was beside Ray on the chesterfield. It had gold wire wings and its head was missing.

When I came into the living room Ray was telling Donny, "You gotta match the colour on the wire at the bottom of the branch with the colour on the pole. Don't ram them in. And the biggest branches go at the bottom." Donny had been putting the tree together upside down.

I gave Ray the letter. He set the tangle of green wire on his lap and read it out loud. I told him about Miss Crans phoning Ma.

With his back to us, Donny muttered, "She sounds like a real bitch." He was ignoring Ray's advice about the right way to put the tree up, instead bending and twisting the fake branches around the pole. They wouldn't stay in place though, sliding down to the base.

"I'll go meet her," Donny chuckled. He turned, grinning at me. "Eh Mikey, 'member that time we nearly ran over your other teacher?" Chuckling, his shoulders rolled beneath his checked flannel shirt.

I sighed, "Yeah."

Ray told me not to worry about it. I got him a pen and he signed it.

"What about this part?" I asked, moving the angel so I could sit closer to him. I pointed to the part where Ma was supposed to pick the time for their meeting.

"Don't worry about it. There's only a few days 'til school's over. By January, she'll forget about it."

"Ray," I pleaded, "she's not like that. Miss Crans ain't like other teachers. She ain't gonna forget—"

That's when Donny went crazy over the fake tree. Throwing branches all over the place, he snapped the pole in two with his knee.

"Fuck this." Part of the pole landed beside me on the chesterfield. Ornaments popped beneath his feet as he stomped out of the living room.

A couple of days later, there was a continuous knocking on our front door. It was early, about a half an hour before I left for school. Ma had gone to work. She left before any of us got up. Ray was in the bathroom. Donny was in bed sleeping with his head under the pillow. Standing on tiptoes, in my long johns and an undershirt, I rubbed a patch of frost from one of the glass squares in the front door. I couldn't believe it. It was her. Miss Crans was on our porch and wouldn't stop knocking.

Her knocking woke up Donny. "Answer the fuckin' door," he hollered from his bed.

I ran to the bedroom. I told him to shut up. I slammed the door.

Pressing my back against it, I put my hands to my head. "It's Miss Crans," I whispered.

Donny sat up, grinning, rubbing course stubble on his chin. He looked wild, his long hair all messy and tangled, and his eyes barely open. Leaping from the end of the bed, he shoved me out of his way. The only thing he was wearing was dirty blue underwear. "Don't worry, Mikey," his voice was gruff, "I'll get it."

Donny stomped toward the front door. I ran to the bathroom to get Ray. Pressing my face into the spine of the bathroom door, I twisted the doorknob but it was locked. The shower was going. Warm fingers of steam crept from between the door and the frame. I begged Ray to hurry up.

The deadbolt on the front door clicked. A rush of freezing air swirled around my ankles as Donny yanked opened the door. At first, Donny began speaking, but Miss Crans cut him off. After that, Donny just listened. I did not know what she was saying, I couldn't hear her, but he stood there in his underwear like a big dumb idiot, like she had him in a sort of trance. It was funny, but it made me more scared of her. Reaching forward, she put her hand over one of the eagle tattoos Donny had on his arm, gently moving him aside. Donny didn't resist. She stepped around him and into the house.

Louder, she stated, "It's a rather chilly morning, don't you think?" Donny nodded, staring at Miss Crans with his mouth open. He was still holding the doorknob. She requested that Donny close the door. When he didn't obey, she placed her hand over his, "Please," she said, closing it herself.

Looking around the house, Miss Crans removed her hat. The fake Christmas tree stood in the living room. She studied it, her eyes taking it in from the stand to the fake angel on the top. Ray and me had finished putting it up. We used grey duct tape to hold the pole together. Some of the fake branches were taped to the pole. The ornaments that Donny hadn't crushed dangled from a branch. Ray had given up on the lights and tossed the tangle of wire under the tree. We had taken yellow wool from Ma's sewing box and wrapped it around the tree a few times. It was supposed to look like fake lights, but it did not. The fake angel sat at the top. I found a Barbie head in the junk drawer and attached it to the angel's shoulders using a pencil as a neck. The pencil was too long and the Barbie's head sat too high from the angel's golden body. When we were done, Ray and me thought the tree looked pretty good, but now that I was looking at it with Miss Crans, I didn't think that anymore.

"Very nice, boys. Did the three of you put it up?" We nodded. By now Ray had come out of the shower and was standing behind me, his hair slicked back and dripping, only a towel around his waist. Miss Crans looked down at me. "Good morning, Michael." She was cheery. "Can I speak a moment with your mother?"

Donny returned to the bedroom without saying another word. I started to tell her about Ma's work, about the letters, but Ray interrupted.

Ray said, "Her shifts are always changing."

"She must come home eventually. I'll come back at the dinner hour then?"

Suddenly Ray remembered something. He snapped his fingers, rolled his eyes. This very morning, he told Miss Crans: "Ma had been looking around the kitchen for a letter I was supposed to have given her." Ray said I was always losing stuff. Before she had left for work, Ray remembered Ma saying something about being late coming home 'cause she had a meeting with Michael's teacher.

"Something about dropping by the school— Today— The day after tomorrow— or Some day— Guess that's to meet with you, eh Miss Crans?"

It was obvious he was making it up. Miss Crans knew. "Yes, I guess that's it. I can count on a visit from your mother, in the class-room, Thursday evening?"

Ray said, "Yep, yep. Thursdays are good—"

Miss Crans didn't let him finish. Pursing her lips she said firmly, "If not, we'll meet again right here, bright and early, Friday morning." She directed Ray to get a pen, a piece of paper. She told him to write down the time she'd be expecting Ma. He had to sit to do this or else the towel would've fallen off.

Her voice became cheery, "And please, Michael, do come along with your mother, I so want you to join us."

She waved her hat in front of her. "Good day, boys." She excused herself and left.

I went into the living room and sat on the chesterfield. Ray stared at the front door, holding the towel closed at his hip and running a hand over his wet hair. He said, "Jesus Christ. What was that?"

I swallowed, "I told you Ray, I told you, she ain't like any other teacher I've ever had."

The night caretaker glanced over the top his newspaper as we passed his office. Even though Ma and me had banged the snow and the salt off our boots, we left wet, dirty stains on the polished tile floor. Outside of the darkened classrooms, students' artwork was taped to the walls. Ma slowed, looking at drawings on purple construction paper. We passed a wall of poems printed in black crayon. There were cut-outs of snowflakes. I had never been in the school this late at night. It was quiet. The only sound came from the heels of our boots scuffing the floor. Somewhere, a telephone started to ring.

"Come on, Ma, Miss Crans is waiting." I took her hand. It was cold. I led her to a stairwell. On the second floor, the caretaker had swept a thin green trail of sawdust down the centre of the hallway. It looked like an unlit fuse. We followed the green sawdust until it led down a darkened corridor, vanishing at the doors of the library.

We went the other way, but Ma stopped. She looked back, following the green line with her eyes. "What's that on the floor for?" she asked.

"It stops the dust from going all over the place when the caretaker sweeps."

"How do you know that?"

"I asked Mr. Young."

"Who's Mr. Young?" Ma started back toward the trail of green sawdust.

"He's the caretaker in the day," I said, catching up to her. I took her hand again. She tried to pull away. "Come on, Ma. It's okay. Miss Crans is waiting."

The door of my classroom was open. Before we went in, Ma asked where the bathrooms were.

"Come on, Ma. They're locked."

Miss Crans sat behind her desk. Ma and me sat opposite on orange plastic chairs. I moved mine closer to Ma's. Neither of us unzipped our coats.

Miss Crans did most of the talking. Sometimes while she was speaking, I'd glance sideways to see what Ma was looking at. Ma looked straight ahead, just a little past Miss Crans. Mostly, I kept my head down, looking at the white crust of salt drying on the toes on my boots. Ma's leotards had a tear in them. Miss Crans wore a pleated paisley skirt. She wore shiny black shoes.

It wasn't until Miss Crans handed Ma a piece of paper that I looked up.

"Have a read, it's short," she said to Ma, "Michael's a fine young storyteller."

Ma's hands remained on her lap. The clock above the door ticked. I never noticed that before.

Waving the paper at Ma, Miss Crans said, "Take it. Go ahead, have a read. I think you'll get a chuckle out of it."

Ma swallowed. "I—" She looked to me. "I must have—" Ma stopped.

Miss Crans leaned forward, setting the paper on the edge of the desk close to Ma.

Ma stared at it for a long time, not saying nothing. Finally, "I forgot my glasses at home."

"Check your handbag."

Ma pretended to look for glasses in her purse.

"I can't find them."

"Here," Miss Crans said, removing the silver chain from around her neck. "Use mine."

She leaned forward, reaching over the desk with the glasses. Ma tucked her legs under her chair, the grit from her boots scraping the floor.

The silver chain dangled from Miss Crans's glasses like a snare. Before Miss Crans could stop me, I picked up the paper and started reading out loud. It was a story I wrote about the time Donny and Ray stuck pears up their teacher's car mufflers.

When I was done, Ma was covering her mouth so we could not see her smiling. Leaning back, Miss Crans folded her arms "Michael," she smiled, "you've got quite the imagination."

Undoing the zipper on my coat a little, I smiled back at Miss Crans.

"And you, Mrs. Hogan, can be proud of your boy. He's a fine lad, just fine."

"I am. I'm proud of all my boys."

Ma and me left the school by the side door. It was snowing. The temperature had dropped. Before we had left the classroom, Miss Crans asked if she could give us a lift. Ma had said, "No, thank you."

When we stopped to cross the road at the lights, I looked back and saw Miss Crans sitting in her car, warming it up. The windshield wipers threw snow off the glass. A snowplow rumbled past. Ma took my hand.

"Where're your gloves, Ma?" Her fingers were cold and turning white.

"I can't remember. I might have dropped them back in the school."

"Let's go back. The caretaker will—"

"No."

The light changed and she hurried across the road, pulling me along behind her.

On the other side, I gave Ma one of my mitts. I put my other hand in my coat pocket. Ma did the same.

Neither of us spoke until near the house. Before opening the door, Ma asked if that story about Donny and Ray and the pears was true. It was, but I told her I made it up. I knew she didn't believe me.

Miss Crans came back to the house one more time. On Christmas Eve. Only Ma and me were home. While she was knocking, I peeked out the window. I didn't open the door. Later, when Ray and Donny came home, they brought in a bag that she'd left on the porch. Donny had bought a bucket of Kentucky Fried Chicken. When he put it on the kitchen table, Ray sat down and opened the lid. He took a piece out, putting it to his mouth. Before he could eat it, Donny made him put it back.

He told Ray, "Let's save it for tomorrow."

The bag was filled with stuff from Miss Crans. Ma came into the kitchen and put on the kettle.

Donny dumped the bag out on the table. There was a brand new pair of ladies' gloves. A fruitcake. A package of ladies' leotards. Two brand new plaid shirts still in plastic. Only one thing in the bag was wrapped in Christmas paper. The label said, *Michael*.

"These must be mine," Ray said, pulling the two shirts toward him, "And this must be for Donny." Tossing the fruitcake toward Donny, it hit him in the chest then dropped to the linoleum with a thud.

"Ray!" Ma said turning from the stove, "Pick that up now," she ordered.

"Yeah Ray, pick it up," Donny chuckled.

I opened the present from Miss Crans. It was a book.

Ray grabbed it out of my hand. He flipped through the pages. "Poetry?" Ray scoffed.

"Maybe the fruitcake's for him too," Donny smirked.

"And the leotards," Ray added.

Ma told them both to be quiet. She told Ray to give me back my present.

The book smelled like leather. It was red and the title was in fancy gold writing. Ma and Donny and Ray all stared at me. I wondered why Miss Crans would give me a book. I would've rather got a shirt.

Ma rubbed her forehead "What's it called?"

I read the title out loud, "*A Shropshire Lad.*"

Under his breath, Donny muttered, "Sounds faggy."

The kettle whistled. Ma made a pot of tea. Ray tried on his shirt.

While she was waiting for the tea to steep, she sat at the table "Read some," she said.

Opening the wrapper on the fruitcake, Donny bit off a piece. "Umm. Rum."

Ray leaned over the table, resting his chin on the back of his hands.

Again, Ma asked me to read something from the book. I opened it and read a line.

At first, I felt sort of stupid, but Ma asked me to keep reading, so I did.

Clay lies still, but blood's a rover;
Breath's a ware that will not keep.
Up, lad: when the journey's over
There'll be time enough to sleep.

Mach I

Donny says Nan's a suck because she cries so much. When Aunt Nora needs a break from taking care of her, Nan lives with us sometimes. She can't do anything for herself. She's senile. She doesn't even know where she is. When Nan's here, she sleeps in Ma's room and Ma sleeps on the chesterfield.

Ma gets her out of bed. Feeds her. Takes her to the bathroom. She washes Nan, too. If Ma's working the afternoon, when I get home from school, I take care of her. If I can't, Ray does. Donny's too rough. He makes Nan cry. If he has to get her up, he'll barge into her room and tear the bedsheet off her. At first she'll get annoyed. When he tugs her out of bed by her bony arm, telling her to hurry up, Nan cries. Donny yells at her to stop it, saying she doesn't have nothing to be crying about. Ma says the way Donny does it, it makes Nan more confused.

The night light makes the bedroom yellow. I turn it on before undoing the buttons on Nan's blouse. Kneeling in front of her, I look away as my fingers undo the final button. I already put the nightie over her head. So I wouldn't see anything, I pulled it down to her shoulders, tugging it, hurrying to cover the front of her. When she is dressed, I look at her again. Her eyes are glassy, the pupils dull. She's confused but lets me undress her for bed anyways. Sometimes she'll call me names of people she must have known a long time ago.

I asked Ma what Nan was like before she went senile.

All Ma tells me is, "She was nice."

I wondered where she came from. Ma doesn't know for sure, but she thinks Nan could have been born in Toronto. Ma said Aunt Nora could tell me more but I didn't want to ask Aunt Nora because she's a real bitch. She's not even our real aunt.

I asked Ma, "When you were a kid, didn't your ma tell you stuff? Stuff about where she was born?"

"No."

"Why?"

"We never asked those types of questions. It just wasn't polite to do so."

For sure, Ma knew that in the forties or fifties, Nan worked at the White Chef on Parliament Street.

"Did she just work there, or, like, did she own it?"

"Just worked there, as a waitress."

Without teeth, Nan's face looks caved in in the middle. It's hard to imagine what she used to look like. I asked Ma to show me a picture of Nan when she was younger. Ma said she'd look, but told me not to get my hopes up because there weren't many photos of Nan when she was a girl. Her parents gave her away when she was eleven or twelve to some people. They gave away her brothers, too, but not to the same people.

Lifting her thin legs onto the bed, I heard the screen door at the back. It was Ray coming in. He was shouting my name. Nan got scared. Whimpering, the corners of her eyes filled with tears. Her pinched mouth opened and closed. When she did this, she reminded me of a fish on land gasping for air.

Thinking someone was coming for her, she took my arm, whimpering softly, "Don't— Don't— Don't— I don't want to go."

I try to calm her. She won't let my arm go. Her nails need to be clipped. They dig into my skin. I tell her it's okay. I brush her hair off her forehead.

I repeat, "It's okay, Nan. It's just Ray. It's okay." It doesn't make a difference. She had no idea who Ray was.

As if he didn't know, Ray called form the kitchen, "Mikey! Where the fuck are you?"

I wished Ray would shut up. Ray came to the bedroom. From running across the yard and into the house, he was panting. Raising his arms, he put his hands above his shoulders, gripping the sides of the door frames. Dropping his chin to his chest, his heavy breathing scared Nan more. With the light on in the kitchen behind him, he looked like a huge spider, or like a bat. Nan pulled her legs up against her chest. I covered her with the sheet.

"Keep it down," I told him.

Ray realized he was upsetting Nan. He shrugged, "Sorry, Nan." Excitedly, he whispered, "Come on, Mike. Leave her. Come out back. You gotta see what Donny's got."

Nan wasn't whimpering anymore. Now she was crying. I told Ray to get out. He told me, "Don't worry, leave her for just a sec. You gotta see this car."

Leaning close, I repeated in Nan's ear, "It's okay. It's okay." Her hair smelled. I told her that Ray didn't mean to upset her. When I turned to get up, Ray was gone. I felt Nan's cheek. It was cold. There was another blanket at the foot of the bed. I covered her. She stopped crying. Her eyes closed. Sitting, I laid my hand on her side. I could feel her ribs, her side rising, falling as her lungs slowly filled, emptied. I stayed a few minutes until I thought she was sleeping.

Outside in the laneway, I heard Ray yell to Donny, "He's coming, He's just putting Nan to bed."

Closing the screen door slowly so it didn't *click*, I could hear Ray speaking fast, but quiet, excited about something. It was almost dark. As I walked through the high grass, the crickets stopped. I had to watch where I stepped because Ray was always leaving shit like old car parts and busted barbeques all over the place. Once, when Donny was high or drunk or something, he tripped and gashed his head open on a rim. We couldn't get it to stop bleeding so we had to take him in a cab to East General. After they stitched up his head, Ma said we had to clear up the yard but we never did.

There was a green Mustang parked in the lane. The hood was open. Donny and Ray were leaning over the engine. A trouble lamp was hooked onto the underside of the hood. The yellow cord snaked across the laneway, disappearing through the fence and into the Chinaman's yard. Ray and Donny were leaning close to the engine. The lamp lit their faces. Ray was pointing at parts of the engine, naming them, telling Donny what's what.

"Hey, Mike. What do ya think?" Ray stopped pointing, waiting to see what I'd say. Leaning under the hood, I put my hand out as though I was going to touch the engine. There wasn't a speck of oil or dirt anywhere on the blue engine block.

"It's hot," I said, feeling waves of heat rising from the valve covers.

Donny said, "No shit." He lit a cigarette, the tip glowing orange. "We just took her for a spin."

I stepped back, taking in the entire car. "It's nice. Where'd you get it?" Neither of them answered.

Donny's brought home a lot of cars. Most of them are busted up shit-boxes. This isn't. Ray reached for the trouble lamp and clicked it off. The three of us stood in the dark. Crickets peeped, filling the night with their calls. Through a tangle of lilac bushes, I could see a soft yellow light from behind the faded sheet covering Ma's bedroom window.

In the darkness, Ray's voice purred as he told Donny and me everything he knew about the Mustang.

"She's a nineteen-seventy-one Mach I Mustang. She's got a four-twenty-nine air ram." He wrapped his arm around my shoulder, pulling me close to him, "Mikey, she'll top end at three-hundred and seventy-five horses. That's a big fifty-six hundred R-P-M's." He said these last three letters slow, like he was twisting somebody's arm. "She's a rocket. Zero to sixty in less than—"

Donny interrupted him, "Unplug the cord. Both of youse get in." He told me to get in the back. Looking inside, I could see there was hardly any room.

"I can't." Donny knew Ma didn't want Nan left alone. I should have checked on her already. I liked checking to make sure she was still breathing.

Donny didn't care. "Get in. We'll go for a quick spin."

Through the gate in the Chinaman's fence, Ray reappeared, the yellow extension cord looped around his elbow and his thumb. Pulling the driver's seat forward, Ray threw the trouble lamp into the back. When I had first come out, I thought the driver's side window was rolled down until I saw bits of broken glass on the bucket seat.

Donny chuckled. "Come on, Ray. Let's go. Mikey says he wants to take her for a spin."

"No I didn't."

Before Ray had a chance to get in behind the wheel, Donny stopped him. "I'm drivin'" he said.

Donny took me by the arm, pulling me toward the open car door. I told him, "Hang on," and ran back to the house.

Opening the screen door might have waked Nan. Instead of going in, I rolled an empty barbeque tank beneath the bedroom window. I balanced on its side. The window was pushed up, held open with a brick. The air was still. The bedsheet curtain didn't move. Pressing my ear against the screen, I listened. No sound came from the bedroom. Behind me, I could hear Donny and Ray. I heard the crickets. There was a gap between the bedsheet curtain and the edge of the window frame. I jumped off the tank, moving it a little so I could see in better.

Nan was only half covered. She must've pulled the blanket off. The yellow night light made her skin paler and her thinning hair less grey. It was difficult to tell if she was still breathing, but her jaw moved like she was grinding her gums so I knew she wasn't dead. Seeing her like this made me not want to go. I didn't want to leave her alone, only half covered up. I knew they'd say no, but I wished I could convince Donny and Ray to stay in the laneway and mess around back there with the Mustang. There was a bag of weed hidden in the basement that I'd been saving. All we'd need were papers. I wanted to go tell them this but my brothers' voices, sharp whispers, called my name through the darkness. Crickets went silent. Jumping off the tank, I told myself Nan would be fine. We'd only go for a spin. Ma wouldn't even know.

When Donny comes home with a car and we boot around in it, we stay on side streets. 'Cause of the cops, we only go for short spins, and after a bit, we dump it someplace.

That's how it started out with the Mach I. At first we stayed on side streets. The car had a lot of power, but Donny could drive anything and he worked the clutch, shifting smoothly. Because his legs were so long, the driver's seat was pushed way back, cramping me even more than I already was. Ray was rifling through the glove compartment, taking stuff out, looking at it, putting it back. He tossed a handful of cassettes back at me. I caught a few, but the rest fell on the floor and on the seat. Donny told Ray to see what he could get on the radio.

We cruised up and down streets crowded with parked cars and people sitting on porches. The Mustang's engine rumbled, throaty, snarling like an angry bulldog. Ray was nervous. A car like this stood out. He spun his head around looking for people looking at us. Even when he was driving, Donny would glance down at his crotch. Steering with one hand, he picked shards of glass from the seat. When he got a piece, he'd look at it for a second and then flick it out the window.

The air was humid with cooking smells from the restaurants and cafés along the Danforth. Donny asked us if we had any money. We said we didn't. Ray had a dime bag and rolling papers, though.

At a stop sign, Donny let the Mustang idle. He said, "Hold on." The tires spun and smoked but the Mustang held back, its rear end swaying, left, right, like a lady's hips when she's dancing slow. When Donny popped the clutch, the Mustang flew. Pushed back into the seat, my ears popped. People leaned over their porch railings and stared from behind screen doors. As we raced past an old Greek man with a thick moustache, he waved a cane above his head, cursing at us in his language. A girl walking a dog tightened her grip on the leash, wrapping the chain around her hand. The dog yelped, confused by the smoke, the screech of tires, the stench of rubber. Leaping toward the road, before it could dart into the street and get killed, the girl yanked the leash, choking the dog but saving its life.

Donny's mouth was wide open. He was laughing like crazy. Ray sat low in his seat, swallowing hard. In a flash we were at the other end of the block.

Idling, the Mustang rumbled. Donny said, "Wicked, eh?" He was ready to go again. Ray looked like he was going to puke. He didn't say anything.

I told them both, "We should get back to Nan." They ignored me.

Tapping the fuel gauge, Donny said, "We need gas. Let's go to Jimmy's."

Ray was quiet. He turned, looking back through the space between the bucket seats. His face was white. He looked as frightened and as confused as that dog we just nearly killed. I wished I had stayed back at the house with Nan. I think Ray did, too.

Jimmy's got three kids. They all work at his Esso. One son, Spiro, is sort of retarded. They're Greek. Their last name has way too many letters in it and sounds like an infection you'd get on your cock. Spiro was named after his dad, but people call big Spiro, Jimmy. The retarded Spiro grew a moustache when he was twelve. I'm not sure if he grew it on purpose. His brother and his sister grew one, too. Their ma wears black. She's not even a widow.

We drove by a few times making sure Jimmy wasn't around. In the summertime, after the station's closed, Jimmy leaves Spiro to sweep and then goes to the Crossroads or the Italian social club to drink with other Greek men. We wanted to make sure Jimmy wasn't around because he has a real bad temper. He's a nut-job, smashing and busting things. He'd shattered about half the square glass windows in the garage's bay doors. If a lug wouldn't come loose or Spiro did something stupid, he'd heave whatever he was holding or whatever was close by, a wrench, a ramp, a lunchbox. He wasn't that big but he could go real wild. Even Donny didn't push him too far.

Spiro's brother and sister work for their dad. They're mechanics. Because he's sort of retarded, Spiro does chores around the station, like sweeping. He can't really do anything else. He's grubby looking, too. Even in the winter, his skin looks suntanned, but it's actually dirt and grease. There's a permanent brownish coating on his face and arms and hands from diving for golf balls in the part of the Don River that runs through the Dentonia Golf course. After a day in the river, Spiro's skin turns the colour of rust. He stinks like a sewer.

A long time ago, Ray used to collect golf balls at the same place with his friend Gordon. Gordon's like Spiro, but less retarded. Gordon and Ray called going into the Don for balls, *pearl diving*. Ray stunk so bad, Donny had to tell him to stop doing it.

We pulled into the station. Spiro was beside a pump. The Mustang sputtered. Donny saved it from a stall. Spiro didn't seem to notice us until we rolled up beside him.

Donny said, "Hey Spiro, your old man around?"

Except for the light coming from the Esso sign, the station was dark. There was a bag of cat litter on its side pouring onto the asphalt. Spiro spread litter with his boot.

Without looking up, he said, "No. Whose car?"

Donny pulled around to the back of the station, shifting into neutral. Opening the door, he got out but then reached under the steering column, messing with wires. The Mustang's exhaust spat a couple of times before the engine died.

When we came around to the front of the station, Spiro held a ten-pound bag of cat litter, dumping it on the ground. The air was sweet with the smell of gasoline. I liked the smell. Donny lit a cigarette.

Spiro pointed at him. "Please stay away from the pumps, Donny please, ten feet please. My dad said so."

Coiling his thick arm around Spiro's neck, Donny led him away from the pumps. Leaning into Spiro, Donny smelled his neck and the side of his head. Donny made a face. "You've been pearl diving, Spiro?"

"Yeah." Cat litter trickled from a hole in the bottom of the bag, collecting around Spiro's heel.

"What did you get?" Donny led Spiro to a row of parked cars waiting to be fixed. A trail of cat litter followed them.

Blinking, Spiro struggled to recall the names. "Some Titlist. Some Spaldings." Dropping the bag of cat litter, he pushed Donny's heavy arm off his neck. Freed of Donny's hold, he spoke quicker, "And. And. And I got one Pinnacle. Sold them all. Where'd you get that car, Donny?"

Before Donny could answer, Ray stepped between them shrugging, he said, "It belongs to a friend of ours. Said we could boot around in it for a while." Taking the pack of Player's from Donny's shirt pocket, Ray slid a smoke out. It dangled between his lips. He offered one to Spiro. A van pulled into the station. Donny walked toward it, waving his arms, telling the driver, "We're closed. We're closed." The van took off.

Ray lit Spiro's cigarette. He lit one for himself. A police cruiser stopped on the street in front of the station. Folding his arms across his chest, Donny stared at the cruiser. Ray told him to relax, have a smoke. The cruiser pulled away.

Donny leaned against a Dodge. Holding his hand out, he angled it until the bluish-white light from the Esso sign wasn't casting a shadow. He picked at a shard of glass embedded in the tip of his finger. I sat on the hood beside him, resting my feet on the bumper.

Ray was talking Spiro up. Asking him about the garage. Telling him about cars. Talking to him about a mechanics course at George Brown he was thinking about taking in September. If Spiro went to Eastern Tech, he'd be in my grade. He goes to a different school. He takes a bus.

Donny was getting tired of hanging around. He interrupted Spiro and Ray. "We got a problem, Spiro—"

Ray got pissed at Donny for cutting in. Donny didn't care. He wanted to get out of here. "We got a problem Spiro. We're low on gas. We don't have any dough—"

Spiro was sort of retarded but he wasn't stupid. He knew what Donny was getting at. He didn't let Donny finish, "I can't," he pleaded, "the pumps are closed."

Donny pushed it, "Couldn't ya—?"

"No. Dad did the dips already. Locked the pumps."

Ray gave Donny a look. Donny went back under the Esso sign's light. He looked for more glass in his hand.

Ray asked Spiro, his voice low, "What about these? Any gas in them?"

There were five or six cars in to be fixed. Shit-boxes, all rusted and dented. By the looks of them, none were worth repairing.

Spiro looked worried. He touched his mouth with the tips of his fingers. "I can't touch them. Dad'll know. He told me to sweep then go home. He said, *Sweep then go home, Spiro.* " He said it like his dad would've, with his Greek accent, eyes tight together, the flesh on his forehead bunching up like rope.

Donny saw what Ray was getting at. Moving out of the light, he came close to Spiro. Real fast, he took a smoke from the pack of Players, bringing his hand up to the side of Spiro's head like he was going to crack him. Spiro winced. I don't think Donny would ever *really* hit him. Instead, he slid a smoke behind Spiro's ear. "That's for you helpin' us out."

Donny was done letting Ray do the talking. He ordered Spiro, "Get me a hose. And an empty gas can."

Spiro was starting to cry. He rubbed his hands together. He looked to Ray.

Softly, Ray encouraged him, "Go on, Spiro. Do what Donny says. Your dad won't even know. "

Spiro's arms didn't move when he walked. They stayed at his sides. The three of us watched him through the dirty windows in the bay doors that hadn't been smashed out and covered with plywood. Light from outside illuminated some of the garage. The rest was shadows. The garage was a mess. A car was up on the lift, one door open a little. There were tools and hoses and car batteries all over the place. Both bathroom doors were marked MEN. Behind a workbench, taped to the cinderblock wall was a centrefold of a naked lady. Beside it was a car calendar marked January 1968. A framed painting of Jesus hung on the wall above the door leading to Jimmy's office. In it, Jesus held a huge, blood-red heart up close to his chest. It was the size a grapefruit. All four fingers on his other hand pointed to heaven. Painted around his head was a black halo, thin as wire. The painting looked like it was taken from a church. The frame was gold. The guy who painted it made Jesus' head too long. It was shaped like an almond.

Moving tools and car parts around in the dark, Spiro banged his head on a motor hoist. He tripped on an air hose. There was a moan as he stumbled and fell against a chest of tools.

Under his breath, Donny called him a fucking idiot.

Ray said, "Give him a break, the guy's retarded."

"So are you."

Ray shrugged.

Rocking the back end of one of the cars, we listened for the sloshing of gasoline but the only sound was the sucking of the shocks compressing. We tried the Dodge. It sounded promising. Donny unscrewed the gas cap, tossing it hard at Spiro. He caught it close to his chest. Kneeling, Donny snaked the end of the hose down the throat of the car's gas tank. He held the other end up toward us. It curved out of the car like a wick.

Donny was looking at Spiro when he asked, "Which one of youse wanna suck?"

Ray and me turned to Spiro. Holding the gas cap at his chest and his other hand waving *no*, Spiro reminded me of the Jesus hanging in his dad's garage. Backing away, Spiro mumbled the warning his dad had given him about not drinking gasoline again.

Donny called us pussies. His cheeks puckered as he drew air from the hose. Before he can get it out, gasoline gushed up the hose and filled his mouth. It spilled down the front him. Spitting, coughing, he had swallowed some but still managed to jam the hose into the red gas can. Steadying himself on the side of the Dodge, he stood, wiped his mouth on the back of his hand and spat. Gasoline poured out of the car like a wound, down the hose, filling the gas can.

When Donny disappeared around the side of the garage, gagging, spitting, Spiro said to me, "You should tell your brother, you should tell Donny Dad said *don't drink gasoline, Spiro*." Like I didn't hear him the first time, he said it again, mimicking his dad, "Mike, *Don't ever drink the gasoline*."

Back on the Danforth, with the gauge on the Mustang's dash at three-quarters full, Donny and Ray and me cruised back and forth, from Broadview to Woodbine. The cafés and restaurants were busy with people lining the sidewalks waiting to get in. Music from other countries blared out of speakers hung above patios. We passed girls tugging at the hems of short skirts, couples strolling hand in hand, leaning against one another. Guys in T-shirts, chests hard as stone, arms as thick as rocks, admiring their reflections in tinted car windows and closed-up shop windows.

At a red light, Donny started showing off. Revving the engine, spinning the tires. Ray told him to quit it. "There's cops all over the place."

Donny said he didn't care.

At Chester, this black guy driving a Nova painted a dull primer red pulled up beside us. Leaning forward so he could check it out, Ray laughed, shook his head, "Fuckin' Nova's all *bondo* and chicken wire."

The light was red. The guy in the Nova revved it.

Donny responded, tapping the gas pedal, revving the Mustang's engine. From the back seat, it felt as if the whole car was being tugged back in a sling.

Green light. Donny was quick on the shift. The Mustang practically left the road, tearing away from the Nova.

At the end of the Danforth, Ray told Donny to go up Broadview. Ray twisted the dial on the radio, stopping at a station playing a song by Boston. Eventually, we snaked through quieter residential streets, trees on both sides, ending up in Leaside, far from where we lived.

Donny pulled into a Dunkin' Donuts. He backed into a spot close to where a bunch of preppy teenagers were hanging out by their cars. Instead of killing the engine to save gas, Donny let the Mustang idle, revving it.

They didn't notice us. I leaned between the seats, reminding Donny and Ray about Nan. The teenagers in the parking lot were dressed in nice clothes. Some of the guys wore cardigans. One was wearing a tie. The girls all wore slacks. Talking quietly, they leaned against New Yorkers, Monte Carlos and BMWs. Windows rolled down, Elvis Costello played on one of the car's tape decks.

Someone said something that must've been funny. They all laughed, tossing their heads back, patting their stomachs. It was hard to tell if they were ignoring us on purpose or didn't even notice we were there.

With the Mustang rumbling beneath us, we watched without talking. One guy, a sharp crease in his trousers, put his hands on his girlfriend's hips, pulling her toward him. They kissed a long time. Donny yanked the wires under the steering column. The Mustang died. Getting out of the car, I stretched, noticing the couple was still kissing.

Donny said, "Let's get coffees."

Inside the Dunkin' Donuts, there were girls seated in a booth. They were pretty, blondes mostly. None of them had on too much makeup. Usually girls noticed Donny because of his height and Ray because of his good looks. These girls didn't.

We ordered coffees. I told Donny and Ray I'd buy. When I did, Ray told the lady behind the counter he'd have a cinnamon-twist, too.

Donny squinted. He said, "Thought you didn't have any money." He slapped the back of my head, but not hard.

I said, "I lied." Ray and me laughed.

Back out in the Mustang, we sat and drank our coffees, talked and watched and smoked. I reminded Donny and Ray about Nan. More cars pulled in. A Firebird, a 'Vette. Music was playing from one of them. It was quiet music, like jazz.

Ray asked, "Where do they get the money for these wheels, eh?"

Donny answered, "From daddys."

Like we're waiting for a show to start, we sat there a while, watching the teenagers standing around their cars. Donny placed his empty coffee cup on the console, careful not to spill the last few drops still in the bottom. Messing around with wires, he said, "I don't wanna sit here listening to this shit. What are they listening to, anyways?"

Ray shrugged, said, "I don't know."

Stepping on the clutch, the Mustang started.

Donny said, "Let's get out of here."

We followed Eglinton to Yonge Street. Doubled back. It was past one in the morning. There were hardly any cars out. Donny hammered it. We got all the greens. streetlights flew past, blurring. We went so fast, it felt like arms were pulling me back into the seat.

At the Don Valley Parkway, Ray said we should start thinking about ditching the car and heading home.

I said, "Yeah," reminding them about Nan.

Donny said, "Nah, we still got half a tank."

We got on the ramp headed north, cutting out of the city going what felt like a thousand miles an hour. The Mustang streaked through the night like a green comet, leaving vans, cars and tow trucks behind in a tail of exhaust.

Light standards on the shoulder of the highway grew further and further apart. Way out in the country at a concession road, Donny exited the highway. As the Mustang went into the curve he told us, "We're low on gas. We won't make it back."

"I thought ya said we had half a tank?"

Looking in the rear-view mirror, Donny chuckled, "I lied."

The coffees were going through us. Donny pulled over, gravel crunching beneath the tires. We got out of the car but kept it running. Side by side by side, we pissed into the gully. I smelled gas from Donny's shirt. Behind us, the Mustang growled, impatient. Far in the distance in front of us, a yellow haze radiated above the city, the black sky bruised yellow.

Ray rolled some joints. We drove more, making jokes about running out of gas. Donny gave me a turn driving. It would've been easier if we weren't high. The Mustang kicked, sputtered. Donny and Ray yelled over each other, "Clutch—Shift— More gas— Clutch—"

We couldn't stop laughing. The car jerked forward ten miles an hour along the pitch-black country road. I had to stop because I was getting a cramp in my side and my eyes were watering from laughing so hard.

The gas gauge was below empty. Donny took over driving again. Not much later, we ran out of gas.

With the hose and gas can from Jimmy's, we got out and walked a little until we came to a gravel lane leading to a farmhouse. A million stars were out, the black sky pinpoints of white. There were no sounds. No dogs barking. No crickets. From road to farmhouse, it was about a quarter mile. Ray whispered, "Mach I would cover that in 'bout eleven seconds."

We walked toward the farmhouse, staying off the gravel so we wouldn't make noise. We didn't talk. We cut across the wide front lawn. My shoes were soaked from dew. There was a Chevy pickup and an Oldsmobile parked by a shed. The cap on the Olds had a lock, but the Chevy's didn't. Donny told me to check out the house, to watch if anyone came out. Carefully, I made my way to the long front porch. Even though they were whispering, Donny and Ray were still too loud. I could hear them arguing about which one of them would siphon out the gas.

There was a light on inside the house. I knew I shouldn't get too close, but I stepped through a garden and peered in the window. The curtains were thin, lacy. In a recliner, below a floor lamp, someone was asleep. I couldn't tell if it was a man or a lady. They were old. They were wearing a thick cardigan. A blanket was covering their legs. A book was propped open on their chest like a tent.

When I got back to the side of the pickup, Donny was spitting out gas. The red container was nearly full. I told him about the person in the chair and asked where Ray had gone to.

"He's messin' around back there." Donny jerked his head, pointing toward the shed. A rattling noise came from the direction Donny had pointed.

Donny whispered, "Idiot's gunna get us shot." He went back to get Ray.

When they returned, I was crouching on the ground. Ray was whispering that farmers have lots of nice tools we could steal. Donny told him to shut up.

As we started back to the road, the porch light came on. We were in the middle of the lawn, in the open. There was nothing to hide behind. No place to run to. Donny and Ray dropped. Ray pulled me down. We lay on our stomachs pressed against the wet grass. I could smell earth and gasoline. Maybe we should have made a run for it.

I heard the lock on the front door. I kept my face down.

A voice called out, so soft it was impossible to tell if it was a man's or a lady's, "Hello? Who's there?" They cleared their throat. Listening, they called a second and third time, "Hello? Hello?" A couple of seconds after the lock was bolted and the light went out, we made a run for the Mustang.

By the time we got back to the Danforth, the sky in the east was a lighter blue. We ditched the car up by East General in an alley and walked the rest of the way home. Along the way, we passed street cleaners and garbage men in bright orange uniforms. Donny and Ray shared the last smoke. At a Coffee Time, we got coffees to go.

Ma was asleep on the chesterfield. Even though she'd be getting up soon for work, we kept quiet. Donny and Ray went straight to bed. Before I did, I checked on Nan. She was on her side, asleep with her mouth open. Pulling the blanket up to her shoulder, I knelt by her face and whispered, "Sorry, Nan," then told her, "Night."

Stepping out of my jeans, I pulled my damp T-shirt over my head. I left the clothes on the bedroom floor in a pile and got into the bed between Donny and Ray's. Even with light coming in through the bedsheet curtains, they were already sleeping.

I closed my eyes but tried to stay awake a few minutes, listening to see if I could hear Nan breathing. In unison, Donny and Ray inhaled, exhaled. Soon, I joined them.

CHIP DIP

Sometimes Ma buys Macintosh apples. They sit in the drawer at the bottom of the fridge. Ma's the only one who eats them. She takes one to work with her lunch. By the time I remember they're there, they're bruised and soft and brown inside. Eventually, most of them go rotten. Ma gets annoyed if she has to throw them out. When Nan stays with us, Ma buys bananas and other soft fruit. The bananas have to be really ripe, black almost, before Nan can eat them because she's got no teeth.

None of us cook except Ma. Most of the time, Donny and Ray and me make our own. In grade eight, everyone has to take home economics, so we know how to make things like fish sticks and grilled cheese. When I don't feel like making anything, or if I have a lot of homework, I'll just eat cereal or a can of pork and beans for supper. At the place where I work part-time as a dishwasher, I get free food. If Manny the cook is working when I'm working, he'll save what doesn't get served and give it to me. He's allowed. It's going to be thrown out anyway.

Through the week, Ma works a lot of overtime. When it's the weekend, Ma's usually too tired to cook. Except for once or twice a week, or on our birthdays, we never eat together. On birthdays, we put money together and buy Chinese food. One year I bought Ma a cake from Dominion with my own money. Ma liked it.

When we eat together, we each have different jobs. My job's setting the table and washing dishes and stuff like that. Donny says he doesn't have to do anything if he doesn't want because he gives Ma the most rent. Ray disappears when it's time to help. He says he has to use the bathroom. For the next twenty minutes, he runs the water and combs his hair until everything's done. Sometimes he disappears down in the basement or takes off to his girlfriend's house.

When Ma does cook, she makes fancy stuff like stew or pork chops with peas and potatoes. Ma knows two ways to make potatoes, boiled or mashed. Mostly, we eat them boiled. They're easier that way. Ma strains them, puts them in a bowl with a little pepper and margarine and they're ready. If she cooks them for too long and they become soft and fall apart, we eat them mashed. I don't care, I like them both ways.

No one's allowed to mash the potatoes except Donny. That's his job because there can't be any lumps. He strains them in the colander, dumps them back into the pot, adds a bit of milk and doesn't stop mashing until every single lump is gone. The rest of the food gets cold, but it doesn't matter. He tells us we have to wait until they're mashed right. He takes so long sometimes, we start eating without him. When he's done, there aren't any lumps, but the masher's all bent up.

Thanksgiving was Ray's idea. Except for the Christmases when Ma's work gave her a ham, we never ate different on holidays. In the morning a few days before Thanksgiving, I heard Ray asking Ma if she was getting the Monday off. She was. He asked if we could eat together then. He asked quietly because he wasn't sure if Donny and me were sleeping. He didn't want us to hear.

Ma was in a hurry. She had to be at the subway station by six-forty-five. She wasn't really listening to Ray as he followed her from the kitchen, to the bathroom. I heard the radio beside the sink click off. The toilet flushed. Ray followed Ma back to the kitchen.

"What do ya think, eh Ma?"

The fridge opened. Ma got out her lunch. "Sure, Raymond. But I gotta go."

Ray said a little louder, "Don't worry. I'll buy the food and help get it ready."

"What? Yeah, okay. Let's talk about it more tonight."

"Ma, I gotta know now. I gotta tell Chantel today 'cause her parents are going away for the long weekend. If she don't come here, she'll go with them."

Ma stopped. "Who's Chantel?"

Ray whispered, "My girlfriend. I told you about her."

"No, you didn't. Listen Ray, I gotta go. Tell your girlfriend, tell Chantel, she can come. We'll have Thanksgiving together. But you'll have to help."

Chantel was older than Ray. She went to George Brown College. She was going to be a nurse. I'm not sure where Ray met her, or what she saw in him. They were completely opposite. Nothing about them was the same. One night in the summer when I was coming home from working, I saw them at Woodbine station. She was wearing a skirt and a white sweater. She hardly wore any make-up. Usually, girls Ray liked were skinny and wore tight jeans and too much mascara. Chantel wasn't skinny, but not really fat, either.

At first, Ray ignored me. Then he tried to not tell Chantel who I was. Chantel stepped in front of him, saying, "Raymond, please. Introduce me."

"This is Mikey," Ray said, swinging his arm toward me.

"Hello, Michael." She held out her hand. "Pleasure to meet you. Raymond hadn't told me he had a brother." By the way she spoke, I could tell she was rich.

Later, I asked Ray about Chantel. He said they'd been going out for a couple of months. He'd even met her parents. "She really likes me," he said, "but don't mention her to Ma, 'kay?" None of us brought girlfriends to the house. Donny never had girlfriends. He just knew some girls.

"So if she really likes you, why don't you want Ma to know?"

"'Cause I just don't."

When Ma had the day off, she slept 'til eight or nine. Nan stayed in bed until one of us got her up. If we didn't, she'd stay in bed all day. The last couple of times she's been with us, she's been getting up and wandering around in the middle of the night. The first time she did it, it was hot outside and the windows were open. Donny thought someone was breaking in. Jumping out of bed, Donny grabbed the baseball bat he kept under his bed and went to see what was going on. I got up and followed him. Nothing ever wakes up Ray.

The house was dark. Yellow light from the street came in through the little square windows at the top of the door. Between the yellow light and the shadows, I could see someone. Their back was to us. The doorknob clicked. The chain rattled. To get a good swing, Donny raised the bat above his shoulder and turned a little. Before he did, I put my hand on his back, "Wait. It's Nan."

Lowering the bat, he turned on the light. While she had been wandering around in the dark, Nan had gone through closets, putting stuff on. On top of her nightgown she was wearing a cardigan and an old winter coat. Over that, she put on her house-coat. She had on two of Ma's winter hats and had tied a scarf around her waist. She was wearing a boot on one foot and a slipper on the other. Nan's real small, but with all this stuff on, she looked bulky, like a scarecrow that had been overstuffed.

"What are you doin', Nan?" Donny yelled, "I was about to smash your head in." Turning, he put the bat on his shoulder and went back to bed.

Ma got up. We took the winter stuff off Nan and led her back to her room. For the rest of the night, Ma said Nan stayed awake. Ma couldn't get her to stop crying.

After that, Ma tried sleeping in Nan's room to stop her from getting up. The next day Ma would be tired, though. Now we just leave Nan alone. We couldn't stop her. Ray said we should tie her to the bed or lock her inside her room. Ma said no. Ma's worried one night Nan's going to fall down the basement stairs. Eventually, she finds her way back to bed. A few mornings we've found her sleeping at the kitchen table wearing clothes that aren't hers.

When Nan goes wandering, we keep sleeping. Not all the time, though. At first, when Nan wakes me up, I think it's mice. We get them sometimes. When it starts getting cold outside, they come in the house. They chew through the side of the box and get into the cereal. I've found mouse shit in the cupboard above the counter. Now we keep the cereal in a plastic container.

In the middle of the night, when the mice wake me up, I think I'm dreaming. They'll chew like crazy and then they'll stop. For a few minutes it's quiet. I'm falling asleep again and the chewing starts all over. Donny put down poison and traps but it didn't make a difference, they always come back. Ray said we should get a cat. The one he brought home smelled. I'm not sure where he got it. It was missing an eye and half its tail. Its shit was like water. It pissed everywhere and didn't catch a thing. Donny got rid of it.

Some nights, I'll wake up and hear Nan in the dining room or the kitchen talking softly to herself. At first, I'm not sure if I'm wide awake or dreaming. It doesn't make sense what she's saying. A lot of the time they're not even words. They're sounds that rhyme or songs she knew a long time ago but forgot the words to. Once in a while, she'll make sense. Then after a couple of minutes, she won't.

All she does is bump into things or turn door knobs or open and close the lid on the old record player in the dining room. Sometimes, she knocks things over. One night, she broke the wing off the carved eagle Ray found in the garbage. He tried to fix it. It was made of wood. After that, the wing kept falling off. He used the wrong glue. Another time, she pushed a chair all over the kitchen, shoving it into the table legs and the other chairs. I'm not sure what she thought she was doing. When I went to get her, she was talking about babies, about giving them away.

It was dark and she didn't know who I was. She didn't get frightened when I took her by the wrist and whispered, "Nan, come back to bed."

Rubbing her thumb and fingers together, her voice was as dry and as thin as an eggshell. As I guided her back to her room, she rhymed, "Cry baby bunting, daddy's gone a hunting, gone to fetch a rabbit skin—" She stopped. I thought she was done and then softly, slowly, she finished, "to wrap the baby bunting in."

I wish she knew who I was. I wish she could say my name.

For most of Thanksgiving Day, it was just Ma and me and Nan at home. Donny left early in the morning. Ray went out after lunch and said he wouldn't be gone long.

While Ma was getting Nan ready, I set the table. The window in our dining room looks across to the window of the house next door. The people who live there never open their curtains. Between the houses there's a driveway. It's too narrow for a car.

I folded paper towels and put them beside each plate. None of the plates matched. All of them were white, but some of them had faded pink roses printed around the edges. On one, the roses were blue. The plates had thin cracks in them that looked like brown hairs. I never noticed these before. In the spot where Chantel was going to sit, I put the plate with the fewest cracks. When I went down to the basement to get an extra chair, I found a box of Christmas party crackers. The box was old. A long time ago, it had gotten wet. The cardboard was rippled and the writing on it was faded. I wondered if they'd still pop when they were pulled apart. Even though it wasn't Christmas, I took them upstairs and put one on each plate to cover the cracks.

Ma told me not to put the plastic cups on the table. I told her the glass ones were scratched and dull. They'd been scrubbed too much.

"Use the glass ones," she said. "Just make sure Chantel's isn't chipped."

There weren't enough knives. Nan didn't need one. Ma cut up her food into small pieces. Ma and me could share, or if he wasn't home for supper, I'd use Donny's.

Ma did all the cooking. Ray didn't help like he promised. He did buy all the food, though. On Saturday night, he came home with groceries. Chicken breasts, Shake 'n Bake, cans of corn, a can of peas, stuffing in a box and a ten-pound bag of potatoes. He even bought gravy. We hardly ever had gravy.

When Ray was putting everything away, I asked him if he had bought dessert.

"Dessert? I bought everything," he said, shrugging "Why don't you buy dessert?"

By the time I got to Dominion, they were closed. I went to Becker's. They don't have cakes like the ones Do-minion had. I bought some fancy cookies and two bags of potato chips. Before I paid, I went to the back of the store where the fridges were and got a tin of French onion chip dip. We don't buy chip dip, so I figured, that'd be like a dessert, too.

When Ma checked the potatoes, they were soft. They boiled too long while she was getting Nan dressed.

"Michael, you're going to have to mash them." She was too tired, she said.

"I can't mash 'em as good."

Ma said she had to finish Nan.

I told her, "But if I mash them, they'll be all lumpy."

"They'll be more lumpy if I do."

I was pouring the water off the potatoes when Ray and Chantel came. The kitchen smelled like cooking, like potatoes before they're peeled. The window at the sink was steamed up. I opened it a little.

As they were taking their coats off, Ray called out, "Hey? Anybody here?" They came into the kitchen. A breeze blew in through the window. It smelled like leaves and fire and wood. Turning, I smiled at Chantel. She smiled back.

"Hello, Mike, happy Thanksgiving," she said, holding up a bottle of wine, "Should I put this on the table?"

Setting the wine on the counter instead, she looked around the kitchen and inhaled. She asked, "What have you been making? It smells good." She was wearing a long denim skirt, a blouse and a red scarf. Ray had on a shirt I'd never seen before. It was orange and had a big collar. The top button was done up. It looked stiff. He was wearing brown dress pants, too. They looked like something you'd buy at Goodwill. Ray never dressed like this. He wore jeans. He wore T-shirts.

Before Chantel could see the potato masher, I covered the handle. Donny had wrapped duct tape around it. The tape had peeled away from being washed too much. Where the sticky parts were, it looked dirty.

Chantel said, "I see you're handy in the kitchen, Mike." There were pots on the stove. Ma had put the chicken on a plate and covered it with foil.

Ray hooked two fingers under his collar and tugged it. The collar was way too tight, pinching his skin. Swinging his other arm in the direction of the stove, he shrugged laughing, "Mikey didn't do any of this. Ma did it, and I bought it all."

Chantel was going to say something but Ma came into the kitchen leading Nan by the wrist.

Ray said, "Hey, Ma. Hey, Nan," then brushed around them and out of the kitchen. Chantel introduced herself. Ma and her talked for a few minutes. While I finished mashing the potatoes, Nan came over and stood beside me. Silver droplets of moisture collected on the windowpane, trickling down the glass and into tiny pools on the sill.

Ma put the chicken on the table and I brought in the potatoes. When Ma and me went back to the kitchen, I whispered, "Why's Ray dressed like that?" Ma whispered back, "I don't know. But don't embarrass him."

While we were bringing the rest of the food into the dining room, Chantel pulled apart the Christmas cracker on her plate. Inside it, there was a green paper crown and a plastic whistle. She unfolded the crown and put it on her head. We did what she did, opening the crackers on our plates. When they were pulled apart, none of them popped, but all of them had a paper crown and a toy inside them. Ma helped Nan with hers. Each crown was a different colour. Mine was red, Nan's was blue and Ma's was white. Ray's was yellow.

Ray started eating. Even without Donny, there wasn't room on the table for everything. After we took our food, Ma carried some of the pots back to the kitchen. When she came back for Nan's plate, she told Chantel and me to start without her. She was going to be a few minutes cutting up Nan's food and making a plate for Donny.

Chantel said, "That's okay, Mrs. Hogan." Placing her hands on her lap, she glanced at Ray, and then at me. "I can wait. We'll all eat together. It's Thanksgiving."

Reaching in front of Nan for the Pyrex measuring cup Ma had used for the gravy, Ray poured gravy on his food. Through a mouthful of chicken, he pointed at the plate with his fork and he reminded us again, "You know, I bought all this."

A few minutes after Ma sat down and we started eating, Chantel remembered the wine. Ray tried opening it with a fork, and then a screwdriver, and then an ice-pick. When he finally got it opened and poured each of us a drink, there were bits of cork floating in our glasses. Ray even poured some in Nan's cup. I only saw Nan drink one other time. That was when Donny and me came home and found her and the old Chinaman who lives behind us finishing off a bottle of Chinese wine. The Chinaman was passed out on the chesterfield. It was hard to tell if Nan was drunk, but her breath smelled like she was. Donny put the Chinaman over his shoulder and dumped him on the broken picnic table in his backyard.

The potatoes were lumpy. I don't like wine but I sipped it anyway. Every so often, Ray would put his fork down and pull at his collar. When Nan chewed, she made a wet, smacking sound with her mouth. The fridge made the humming noise I usually only heard at night. When we first started eating, no one hardly talked except for when Chantel said how tender the chicken was and when Ma thanked me for my help when she was getting Nan dressed. As I was picking a piece of cork off my tongue, Chantel asked how old I was, if I was allowed to drink. Glancing at Ma, I shrugged, "Sort of."

Ma leaned back and laughed, "Sort of? What does that mean?"

I shrugged again and all of us laughed. Ray finally undid the top button on his shirt.

Chantel filled Ma's glass with more wine. She asked Ma about work. Ma told us a funny story about a Portuguese cleaning lady she worked with once who asked why we celebrated a holiday called *Thinks*giving. Ray told a joke about a turkey, a fox and a Jewish guy but ruined it because he couldn't remember the ending.

As Chantel was filling her glass with more wine, she asked Nan, "Do you know any jokes, Nan? Would you like more wine?"

Instead of answering, Nan rhymed words together. She said something about a baby and a water pump. Setting her fork down, she made a whimpering noise. Her bottom lip trembled. She rubbed her thumb and fingers together. Listening to her as if she made sense, Chantel set the bottle down and leaned closer to Nan. Nan stopped crying and rubbed her fingers against Chantel's cheek.

Nan asked, "Who are you?"

Chantel spoke slow, as though Nan was normal, answering, "Well Nan, my name is Chantel Sallis. I'm twenty-three years old, and I study nursing. Eventually, I'd like to work in a neonatal care unit." As she was speaking, Chantel took Nan's paper towel and used it to wipe off a piece of corn that was on Nan's chin.

Chantel told Nan her parents wanted her to become a doctor, but she didn't want to go to school for the rest of her life. She had an older brother named Mac who was a fourth-year medical student at McGill.

She said, "By the time he's prepared to practice, he'll be an old man."

Ray interrupted, "McGill? What's that?"

Chantel answered, "It's a university in Montréal."

"Oh."

Chantel took a sip of wine then dabbed her lips with her paper towel. Even though she was directing everything at Nan, Ma and me stopped eating and listened. Ray kept scoffing his food down.

Chantel told Nan about places in the world she'd been to, places I'd never heard of. She told Nan, wherever she went, she took photographs of the stuff she'd seen.

She said, "I might not ever get back to see it again."

She was quiet a moment, then glancing at Ray, she told us how she liked trying new things, different things than what she was used to.

In her house, she had a darkroom. "One day, I plan on having an exhibit. A friend of my parents owns a gallery in Caledon. There are a lot of other things I want to do too."

Leaning forward, Ma asked, "Like what?"

"Well, I'm going on a—"

Before she could finish, the back door opened. It was Donny. I wanted to hear where she was going but she stopped talking when Donny came into the dining room. He didn't sit down.

While we had been eating and talking, it had gotten dark outside. Turning on the light above the table, Donny didn't say anything, he just looked us looking at him. There was a cut above his eye. It was swollen. The blood was dry. None of us asked what happened. Looking around the table at the others, I remembered my paper crown. Slowly, I raised my hand and touched it. Chuckling, Donny stared at Ray. "Hey Ray, why you wearing that shirt? You look like a fuckin' punkin'."

"Donny!" Ma said, glancing at Chantel. "Get your dinner, it's in the oven."

While Donny was in the kitchen, Ray cleared his throat a couple of times. He did up the top button on his shirt. Turning to Chantel, he sat up and grinned. "Now that we're all here, we have an announcement."

Chantel looked from Ma, to Nan and then at me, waiting for one of us to say something.

Waving two fingers back and forth between him and Chantel, Ray said, "Not them. Us. *We* have an announcement."

"We do?"

"Yeah," his voice cracked, "we're getting married."

"What? We're what?" Chantel put her hands on the edge of the table and pushed her chair back.

Donny came into the dinning room with a plate of food. He sat across from Ray and without looking up said, "Knocked 'er up, eh Ray."

"Donny!" Ma shifted in her chair.

Chantel raised her hand, "It's okay, Mrs. Hogan." She turned to Donny and said, "No, I'm not." Shaking her head, she told Ray, "And no. We are not getting married."

"Married—" Nan said. She smiled so wide her gums showed. Donny picked up a chicken breast, and as he pulled meat off the bone with his teeth, Nan began to clap. Fingers curled closed, the flesh on the back of her hands seemed almost transparent. Raised knuckles and bones in her wrist moved like small, hard marbles.

Nan sang softly, "*I love you truly, truly dear, life with its sorrows, life with its fears, fade away when you are near, I love you truly, truly dear.*"

Closing his eyes, Donny shook his head. Under his breath he moaned, "Jesus Christ." The rest of us stared at Nan, waiting to hear if she was through. Donny put a forkful of potatoes in his mouth and chewed. "Holy shit," he said out loud, "who mashed these?"

"Donny!"

Chantel told Ray again, "We're not getting married."

Ray asked why not.

"There are *things* I want to do still. Don't you listen? I've got plans for when I've finished school." Crossing her arms, she added, "I might not ever get married."

Ray pulled the paper crown off his head, tearing it. He crushed it into a ball. Sighing, he asked, "Things like what?" He tugged at his collar, but this time, the top button popped off. It landed in the gravy, slowly sinking through the skin which had formed on its surface.

Chantel explained, "*Things* like what I've been saying to your Nan, *things* like when I'm done school, I want to go to Sierra Leone or maybe New Guinea."

Using his fork, Donny squished lumps out of his potatoes. With his other hand, he pressed the cut above his eye to feel if it was bleeding.

"Why?" Ray asked. "Where's that, anyways?"

Dropping the fork into his plate, Donny snapped, "Listen Ray, you fu—"

"Donny!"

"Ya goof. It's simple. You got a ring for 'er? No? Then you're not getting married. Besides, girls like her don't marry people like us. Now shut your mouth, I'm tryin' to eat."

Rolling the crushed paper crown in the palm of his hands, Ray sat there, looking at it and not saying a thing.

Putting a forkful of corn in his mouth, Donny grinned, "Is that why you're dressed up like that? So she'd say *yes*?" When Donny chuckled, half-chewed kernels flew out of his mouth, landing on Ray's orange shirt. All of us laughed a little. Chantel covered her mouth, but I could tell she was smiling.

Nan got out of her chair and wandered around the dining room. She went to the old stereo and opened and closed the lid. She rhymed words and hummed. A few times she said the word *married*.

Chantel started to get out of her chair. "You want to hear some music, Nan? Do you like to dance?"

Donny made a fist and banged the table. Glasses and plates rattled. Chantel stopped. We all sat up. Pushing his chair back, he clenched his teeth and said, "We don't dance." He got up and left the dining room with his plate. Fresh blood oozed from his cut.

Opening and closing the lid faster, Nan started whimpering. Like nothing happened, Ma pushed her chair away from the table and picked up her plate. Pretending to smile, Ma said to Nan, "It's okay, Nan." Ma said to the rest of us, "I'm stuffed. Think I'll put the kettle on. Would you like tea, Chantel?"

I added, "There's coffee, but it's instant."

From the kitchen, Ma called out, "Mike, is there any dessert?"

Ray carried his fork and plate to the kitchen and set them in the sink. Nan wandered around while me and Chantel helped Ma clear the table. Ray said he'd help clean up but first he had to use the bathroom. For the next twenty minutes, he ran the tap and pretended to be taking a shit. I could hear the show Donny was watching in the living room. The TV was turned up too loud.

The kettle whistled. Ma made a pot of tea. As she was pouring the water, Ma asked Chantel what she was going to do in those places she had mentioned.

"In New Guinea? I'm going to do work with CIDA." While we went back and forth between the kitchen and the dining room clearing the table, she told us what CIDA was and about another agency she'd volunteered for called OXFAM.

When me and Chantel were alone in the kitchen for a minute, I wanted to tell her I was sorry about the way Donny acted. I did not. When the tea was steeped, Ma took the pot and put it on the table. When she came back for the milk and the sugar, Ma asked Chantel to get the cups and some spoons. As I was wiping grease off the counter, I heard Ma whisper, "You know Chantel, you wouldn't wanna to marry a guy like Ray. They never help clean up." Both of them laughed.

Opening the cupboard below the sink, I reached for the dish rack but Ma stopped me. "Leave them," she said, "Let's have tea first. Did Ray get dessert?"

"No, I did."

Nan's tea was too hot. Ma didn't give it to her. She sat Nan down and told her she'd have to wait. I opened the fancy cookies. In the cupboard where the cereal was, I found a bowl big enough for both bags of chips. As I was dumping the second bag in, I remembered, I hadn't checked for mouse shit. I put the bowl and the chip dip in the middle of the table.

The tap went off in the bathroom. Ray came out and went into his room. He came back to the dining room in jeans and a T-shirt. He saw the dessert and asked who bought it.

Sinking a chip into the dip, Chantel put it in her mouth. She said, "Mike did."

"Chips and chip dip? That ain't dessert."

She reached into the bowl and took a handful of chips. "It is tonight."

Before Ray went into the living room, he asked Chantel if she wanted to watch TV. She didn't answer.

After Ray was gone, Chantel leaned forward, lowered her voice and asked, "What's wrong with Donny?"

Ma shifted in her chair. "Nothing." She picked up her cup and brought it close to her mouth. Instead of taking a sip, she blew over the rim. "Probably just cut himself by accident."

We drank our tea and talked. I turned off the light above the table and turned on the floor lamp in the corner. Chantel asked me about school. She asked what my plans were when I graduated.

"Get a job or something."

"You ever think about going to university or to college?"

I looked at Ma. "No. Well yeah, sometimes."

Nan sipped her tea. She got up and walked around us. She went into the kitchen for a few minutes.

Chantel asked Ma about the other jobs she'd had. She asked Ma where she grew up. I learned stuff about Ma I never knew before.

Nan wandered into the dining room. She went to the stereo and opened and closed the lid on the turntable. Ma went to the kitchen to make more tea.

"I think your Nan wants to hear music," Chantel said. "Nan, do you want to dance?"

Finishing her tea, Chantel went over to the stereo and said something to Nan too quiet for me to hear.

Taking a bite of a cookie, I told Chantel, "The record player part doesn't work. It needs a new belt."

"How about the radio?"

"That works, I think."

Chantel pressed the power button. Nothing happened.

"Maybe it's unplugged." I checked. It was. I plugged it in. The radio came on, blaring loud. The volume had been turned up to ten. The DJ's voice was distorted. It startled Nan. She took a step backward. Chantel turned the volume down and twisted the dial until she found a station playing music.

Chantel gently took Nan's arm as though she was going to dance with her, but instead she moved Nan toward me.

"Dance with her."

"With Nan?"

"Yes."

I wanted to go back to the table, to sit down and have more tea. Looking at my feet, I said, "I don't even know this song,"

Chantel put her hand on my back and nudged me and Nan together. "Come on, Mike."

"But I, I don't know this song."

"It doesn't matter. Come on Mike, it'll make your Nan happy."

"But I—"

"It's The Commodores. Come on, dance with her. The song's almost over."

Biting my lip, I said quietly, "I never danced before. I don't know how."

Suddenly stepping in front of Nan, Chantel stood close to me. She took my hand and put it around her waist. I could feel the curve at the bottom of her spine. She took my other hand and pulled me forward. The front of us almost touched. With her hand on my shoulder, she pulled me into her. I was taller than her. I didn't know where to put my face or how close to put my head to hers. When our crowns touched, they made a sound like wrapping paper being opened. I smelled shampoo. Her hips moved.

Mine didn't. Against my chest I could feel the roundness of her breasts. I swallowed. My mouth went dry.

Nan stood watching, smiling.

The kettle whistled. The song ended. Another song began.

When Chantel spoke, her lips almost touched my ear. "See," she whispered, "you're doing it right now."

"Doing what?"

Before she could answer, Ma came back with the tea. We stepped apart. Pretending she hadn't noticed anything, Ma said she didn't realize how late it was. Tomorrow was a work day. She still had to make lunch and get Nan ready for bed.

After another tea, and some cookies and chips, Chantel said she had to go. She went to the front closet. I thought she was going to tell Ray she wanted to leave. Instead, she came back to the dining room with her coat and her purse.

Taking off her paper crown, she carefully folded it and slipped it in a pocket in her coat. From the middle part of the purse, she took out a small camera. She asked if she could take a picture of us. Ma said okay, and then told me to get Ray.

As I was about to get up, Chantel put her hand around my wrist and stopped me. "Not him," she said, "just the three of you."

We stood by the window. Chantel looked through the lens. She said if the light wasn't right, the picture wouldn't turn out. She moved us. She sat Nan in a chair. Ma stood on one side and I stood on the other. As Chantel held the camera up, I heard her say to herself, "Needs more light."

Turning on the light above the table, she looked through the camera again and told us to smile, to say cheese. Out of the corner of my eye, I saw Ma smile. After the flash, Nan said something, but I wasn't sure what.

Putting the camera away, Chantel thanked Ma for everything. They hugged. Ma told Chantel Ray would walk her to the subway.

"It's okay, Mrs. Hogan. Let him watch TV. I drove us here."

QUIET AS INDIA

Ray came home Saturday morning with twenty loaves of bread and a rhubarb pie. Ma was at work already. Before Donny and Ray started eating it, they cut a piece of pie for Ma and put it on a plate in the fridge for her to have later. They were eating the rest with spoons and drinking milk when I came into the kitchen. Loaves of bread were on the counter and the floor and on top of the stove. I don't like rhubarb pie. I got a fork and sat at the table and ate some for breakfast anyway.

Ray was excited, talking fast. "There's tons of bread, trays piled this high." Straightening his arm, he held his hand above his head. "Not just bread and pie either, there're muffins and buns and waffles, doughnuts and bagels. Gordie took doughnuts. I told him to take other stuff but he said his ma loves those little doughnuts with the white powder on 'em. That's all he wanted to take for 'er."

Ray scoffed down more pie. He tilted the carton of milk to his mouth and gulped. "All the times we've been hacking around behind Dominion, it's never been there until now. All this free food just sitting there waitin' for us to take it. Gordie and me are going back tomorrow morning."

The night before, Ray had slept at Gordon's. Since he was twelve or thirteen, Ray's slept at Gordon's on Friday nights and Saturday nights. They actually didn't sleep. They'd go out and do shit. Even though Gordon's allowed to sleep at our place, he's never wanted to. He did only once. Donny scared him so bad, he had to go home in the middle of the night. Ray and Gordon were sleeping in the living room. They were about fourteen. Donny came home a little boozed up. Gordon woke up to Donny's knee pressing down on his chest and his hands around Gordon's throat. Donny was acting like he was strangling him. The whole time he was laughing but Gordon was terrified. He peed the chesterfield. The next time Ma saw Mrs. Daniels, she apologized for what Donny did to her son.

Donny took a drink from the carton. He wiped his mouth with the back of his hand. "Don't waste your time. Dominion's closed Sundays."

"So? The bread might still be there."

Donny called Ray a goof. "Weston's makes deliveries before stores open. You and Buttfuck got there early before anyone was there to take the trays inside."

Ray dragged two fingers along the bottom of the foil plate, scooping bits of piecrust and rhubarb into his mouth. "Fuckin' right it was early. It was still dark, five or five-thirty. I haven't even gone to bed yet."

For a couple of summers when Donny was still in school, he worked at the Weston's plant on Carlaw. For a while, he worked there full-time. When I was kid, I used to wait by the loading doors for his shift to finish. The plant was huge. It smelled good, too. Workers were allowed to have day-old bread for free. On the way home, Donny would let me light his cigarette and while he smoked, I'd eat soft slices of Wonderbread.

The rhubarb pie was done. Ray licked the foil. We made toast. Donny told Ray not to go to the back of the Dominion with Gordon. "Don't take anything else."

Ray asked, "Why not?"

Donny said "Just 'cause."

Donny had started working for a landscaping company in the spring. At the beginning of the summer, him and Ray and me had gone down to the hiring trailers inside the Princes' Gates on the Exhibition grounds to apply for jobs. They hired us, but the jobs didn't start until the Ex opened in August. You needed a Social Insurance Number to work. You had to be sixteen to get one. Around March, Donny got me the form and told me to fill it out. He said I should've done it a year ago. Just before school finished my card came in the mail. Up to now, I'd only ever worked for cash. The Ex would be my first real job.

In the meantime, we made money selling the Wonderbread and pies and doughnuts we took from the back of Dominion. People around the neighborhood were our customers. Eventually, we sold them milk, too.

The first time we went for bread, Donny shook me awake. He said, "Get up. Get dressed. Don't wake Ma." Sitting up, I rubbed my eyes. Ray was in the bathroom taking a piss in the dark with the door open. It was three-thirty in the morning.

Outside, the air was cool, sweet smelling. Somewhere close, a dog kept barking. Most of the cars on the Danforth were taxis. The police cruised by us going slow. Donny told Ray we should take side streets. I had to hurry to keep up. We walked the whole way, but we walked too fast and got there too early. No bread had been delivered yet.

To stay out of the light from the parking lot's lampposts, the three of us crouched behind a garbage bin. There was broken glass and gooey shit all over the asphalt. The bin was full. It reeked. The lid was open. Dominion throws out a lot of rotten produce, like lemons and melons and pears. Covering his nose and mouth, Ray whispered, "Let's close the lid." Donny whispered back, no, doing that would make too much noise. While we were waiting, raccoons came sniffing around for something to eat. Donny scared them away with a broken hockey stick.

When the Weston's bread truck finally came, the sky was getting light. Leaning against the cool steel side of the bin, I had dozed off. Donny jabbed me in the ribs. The delivery man took a few minutes to unload the bread. For ten minutes after that, we watched him sitting in the cab with the inside light on, sipping coffee and flipping through papers attached to a clipboard. On either side of me, I could hear Donny and Ray's stomachs making noises. I was hungry, too. By the time the bread truck started and pulled away, we were too tired and it was too light out to take anything.

The whole way home, Donny walked ahead of Ray and me. He was pissed off at himself. It was like someone had cheated him or tricked him. Swinging the broken hockey stick he'd used to scare the raccoons, he'd say *fuck* out loud and kick at nothing on the sidewalk. Near the house we passed Ma on her way to the subway. She was surprised to see us, but didn't have time to ask what we were doing.

For the next couple of mornings, Donny went by himself. By the time he'd come back, Ma had gone to work. We'd sit at the table in the kitchen and make plans. He told us we were going back. Five the next morning, he shook me awake.

"Get up. Get dressed. Don't bring your wallet or any ID. Hurry up. Ma'll be up soon." I got up, put on pants, went to the washroom and closed the door. I took a piss in the dark.

The clock in the kitchen said five after five. "It's too late," I whispered, starting back for bed, "By the time we walk all the way there, it'll be six."

Grabbing me by the arm, Donny whispered back, "Let's go. We ain't walking."

Out back in the laneway Donny had a van. There were no windows on the sides or the back. Ray was sitting in the passenger seat smoking. I got in the side. Before sliding the door closed, I looked around inside the van. A small light bulb hung on a metal clip. The smell of detergent and bleach was so strong, it made my eyes water. I sneezed. Cars Donny brought home were never *this* clean. Donny had power-washed the whole inside of the van.

We crossed Woodbine and pulled into the parking lot behind Dominion. Reversing, we parked beside the garbage bin, facing the back of the store. Donny turned the engine off. The bread had been delivered. Beside the trays of bread, a column of milk crates were stacked six high.

It was still dark out, but the sky was getting lighter. Waiting for Donny to tell us what to do next, we watched the bread and the milk like something was going to happen to it. None of us spoke. When Ray went for a cigarette, Donny told him no, have a smoke later. The quiet made me a little nervous. If I was with other guys, my heart would be pounding out of my chest by now. Because I was with Donny and Ray, it wasn't.

Ray was impatient. "Let's go. Let's get it. What are we waitin' for?"

At the top of the rusted lampposts that edged the empty parking lot, stout, pear-shaped bulbs cast cones of yellow light over the pitted asphalt. Suddenly, they flicked and turned off, but not completely. As the light faded, their circles of yellow shrinking, it looked as though the bulbs were working in reverse. Instead of throwing light down, now they absorbed it, drawing it up into the lampposts and away. Dimming before our eyes, for a few seconds before the light vanished completely, the bulbs' filaments glowed, red-hot and electric. The parking lot was dark. Ray looked worried. Donny said, "Don't worry. That's what we were waiting for. They're on timers." He looked at his watch "Sunrise is in twelve minutes at 5:33." Kneeling on the floorboards between Donny and Ray's seats, I shifted my weight, from one knee to the other. I asked how he knew when the lampposts would turn off. How he knew the exact time the sun rose.

"I checked before," he said, "but there's one more thing we gotta wait for."

Ray didn't want to wait no more. He wanted to get the van loaded right now and split. His voice cracked when he said, "Fuck, Gordie and me just came along and took it. We didn't wait for nothin'."

"You guys were just lucky. And stupid—" Donny stopped. The store's air conditioning units clicked on. Circulation fans began to whirr. A humming, high voltage drone startled the pigeons which nested under the building's overhang. Two circulation fans were mounted on their sides on a steel platform. Each fan had four blades about six feet in diameter. As the blades gained momentum, their electric motors grew louder. At top speed, they looked like propellers, spinning so fast you couldn't even see them. Sitting in the van listening to them now, they seemed louder than during the day.

By now, it was half-light outside. Ray rubbed his knees and looked all around. Donny told me to get out of the van. As I did, he instructed, "Walk to the corner of the parking lot. Make sure you *walk*. Act normal. Ray and me are going to get the bread—"

Ray cut in, "—And the milk?"

Donny told him to shut up. He said, "Listen Mike. If you see police, make a noise. Act like you're calling your dog." Donny put two fingers to his mouth, pretending to whistle. "*Come 'ere Buddy, here boy.* Something like that. Make sure you're loud so we can hear it over the fans. Okay?" Reaching into his jean jacket, he pulled out a dog leash. "Here. Take this. It'll make it look real." Twisting the leash around my hand, I nodded and Donny nodded back. He smiled a little, reassuring me, "Don't worry though, the cops ain't going to come. When you see us pull away, cross Woodbine and *walk* down Ventor to Connery Pool. We'll pick you up there, okay Mike?"

Swallowing, my heart beat a little faster. Donny stressed, "Whatever you do, don't ever run. They'll come after Ray and me and the van, so you gotta just walk away from us. Understand?"

Now I was more scared, but I was too afraid to show it. I repeated his instructions, "So, if the cops come, I just walk away? Leave you guys—?"

Turning, Ray interrupted, "Yeah, and don't forget to whistle. Don't forget you're walkin' a dog. Now get going."

I looked at the leash. "But I don't *have* no dog. I don't know how to whistle."

Ray rolled his eyes. "That's the point, ya idiot. And shit, anyone can whistle. You're just out walkin' Buddy but he took off from you. Now you're looking for 'im. That's all."

When I was halfway across the parking lot, the van started. I glanced back. Over my shoulder the horizon was crazy with colours, yellow, orange and red. Watching for police, I did just like Donny told me, waiting until the van was loaded and they pulled away, then I walked in the direction of Connery Pool. I practiced whistling. After a while, I felt stupid calling out "*Buddy, here Buddy*" so I stopped.

At the path that veered from the sidewalk toward the pool, there was a green wooden sign. It was engraved with the name

Ethel Mills-Connery Field. Other words and names had been carved in the sign. I recognized a few. Gordon and Ray's were the biggest. In the uncut grass below the sign, weeds sprouted. Dandelions pushed up through whitish-brown clumps of dried dog shit. Beyond a row of trees, set back from the street, the pool was enclosed by a high, chain-link fence.

Every time a breeze picked up, the smell of chlorine blew in my face. In the day, when it was open, you entered through the blue turnstile that led to the change room doors. At this hour, the only way in was over the fence. Branches that had grown over onto the pool side had been cut back. Hovering above the pool like spirits, patches of mist rose out of the flat and still water. Sunlight flashed off its surface. Watching for the van, I dropped the leash and sat on the wet grass. From where I was leaning against a tree, I could see both the pool and the street. Only once did I think about Donny and Ray getting caught.

Connery Field was big. It was named after an alderman or a dead mayor of East York. Besides the community centre and the outdoor swimming pool, there was a baseball diamond, two soccer fields with football goalposts, tennis courts and a wall, used for handball, covered in graffiti. Every firecracker day, fireworks were set off in the middle of the baseball diamond. A long time ago, I think Ma pulled me there in a wagon to see them. I remember it getting dark and the crowds but I can't remember the fireworks going off. Mostly, the people waiting for the fireworks to start were white or Greek or Italian. A lot of them had brought lawn chairs. It was like a party with music, people laughing and a man playing a little guitar. Families sat on blankets. Couples lay on the hoods of cars, leaning against the windshield, holding hands, waiting, watching the darkening sky. Ma and me sat far away from everyone. Maybe it started raining. Maybe it got too late and Ma pulled me back home before the fireworks started. I can remember so much from that night, but I can't remember the sky being lit up, the *boom* and colours of the fireworks.

Donny and Ray were taking longer then I expected. It was still early, but it was daylight now. A man jogged into the park with his dog trailing him. People were going to work. Cars drove by. The water in the pool rippled, moving as though something small had fallen into it. A minute or so later, the surface was smooth once again, sunlight glinting through the thinning vale of mist. Down the street, a taxi stopped. I stood, stretched. My stomach made noises. What was taking Donny and Ray so long? I thought about them getting caught. Again, the water in the pool was disturbed, ripples troubling its reflective surface. This time though, I saw something. It was black. Maybe a squirrel had fallen in. Leaning against the fence, I could see something swimming below the surface. Someone was swimming underwater. The whole time I'd been waiting for Donny and Ray, someone had been in the pool.

I stood on tiptoes and pressed my face into the fence. Hooking my fingers through the wire, I pulled myself up a little. At the far end of the pool, the swimmer came up for air, breathed, quietly submerged. Beneath the water, the swimmer turned, pushed off the wall and in a burst, started toward me. To get a better look, I climbed a tree and hid amongst the leaves. From up here, I can see to the bottom of the pool. The swimmer was a lady. She was wearing goggles. Her bathing suit was the colour of flesh. Nearly the entire length of the pool, she didn't come up for air. I could only see the back of her. Like water flowing over stones, her long dark hair, her entire body slipped through the water, sleek, smooth. Arms sweeping, legs thrusting, quiet as a thief, she propelled herself forward. Adjusting my weight on the branch, I wondered if she knew I was here. I wondered if she knew I was watching her.

I heard the van. I saw it through the leaves roll up to the curb and stop. Without getting out, Donny and Ray looked around. I wished they hadn't come just yet. I wanted to keep watching. I wanted to find out who the swimmer was. I don't know why, but I didn't want Donny and Ray to know about her.

If I didn't climb down, I knew they'd get out and look for me. I hopped down out of the tree. At the van, I slid the door open and got in. It was filled with trays of bread. Donny put the van into gear. We pulled away. Because there were no windows at the rear of the van, I couldn't look back, but in my head, I imagined my swimmer. By now, she'd have swum another length.

Without turning Ray said, "Eh Mikey, did *Buddy* get stuck up a tree?"

He flicked a butt out the window and laughed.

Trying to act normal, I didn't tell him what I was doing in the tree. Instead, I asked, "What took youse so long?"

Ray replied, "Donny wanted to boot around for a while."

I asked how it went loading the bread. I didn't say anything about the swimmer. At a stop sign, Donny reached back and said, "Pass me up a loaf, will ya, I'm starving."

I handed him a Wonderbread. Steering with his knees, he removed the plastic tab and set it on the dashboard. He took the top three slices. With his mouth full, he said, "Here Mikey, take some. I can hear your fuckin' stomach from up here."

He chuckled. Ray laughed. Smoke blew out of his nose and mouth. He had been lighting another cigarette.

At the next stop sign, Donny turned and looked at me. "Somethin' wrong, Mike?"

I looked down. "No."

Lowering his voice so Ray couldn't hear, he sort of smiled and said, "You saw India, didn't ya?"

"Who?"

"India. Ya know, Tim's daughter."

"Tim?"

"Yeah, ya know, *Pop-Bottle* Tim. India was in the pool, wasn't she?"

I was going to lie. Donny could tell if I was, so I didn't. "Yeah. How'd ya know?"

"She's there alotta mornings."

Ray wanted to know what we were talking about.

Donny told him, "Nothin'."

Donny passed me the Wonderbread. He started driving again. I took out a slice. It was soft. It stuck to the roof of my mouth.

We didn't go every morning. When we did, we'd do it the same way. Ray wanted Gordon to come. Donny said no, we don't need him. Ray said Gordon could do what I was doing, acting like I was looking for my dog, and to make it more real, he could bring his wiener dog.

Donny squinted, he shook his head. "Why the fuck would he be lookin' for his dog if he's got it right there with 'im? Anyways, Buttfuck ain't allowed in Dominion." Donny chuckled.

Ray got a little pissed off, shooting back, "That was a long time ago."

Donny was talking about when Mrs. Daniels got caught stealing. Since she got caught shoplifting from Dominion, Gordon hasn't been allowed in the store. If he tried, the manager went after him with a short club and chased him away. Donny said only welfare cases shoplift.

Donny hadn't noticed I wasn't bringing the leash anymore. I couldn't find it. The other thing he didn't know was, in hope of seeing India swimming underwater, I was practically running to the pool in Connery Field. She was there, but not all the time. I found a better tree to see her from. It was on the opposite side, by the diving board, away from the street.

After a couple of days, Ma asked where the bread was coming from. Along with the loaves of Wonderbread, pies and bagels and doughnuts were piled on the chairs and two card tables Donny had set up in the dining room. There was more on Donny's bed. She didn't know about those, though. We kept the door closed. Donny told her he was getting it from Weston's, from a guy he used to work with.

"It's all day-old stuff, Ma. They gotta get rid of it." Ray and me stood behind him in the kitchen, nodding.

She didn't believe us. I could tell because she didn't say anything else. When Ma wasn't around, I asked Donny and Ray how come Dominion didn't notice that their bread was disappearing. We were sitting around the kitchen table. Ray was making toast.

Donny said, "'Cause we don't take it all."

Ray added, "And 'cause Donny's changing the waybills. A guy at Weston's gave him a bunch of—"

"Eventually," Donny cut in, "they'll figure it out, and once we start taking milk, *if* we're not careful, it'll be a matter of time before we're caught."

"So we shouldn't touch the milk then, right?"

Licking margarine off a butter knife, Ray scoffed, "Yeah we should, and we should've started taking it already—"

Donny didn't let him finish. "Listen, we're gunna get milk. Just like the bread though, we gotta know when to start takin' it and when to *stop* takin' it."

We didn't take milk until Donny got a fridge. He spent a day cleaning it. He put it in the backyard out of the sun and plugged it in with extension cords. So it wouldn't be noticed or get ruined if it rained, he covered the front and top with a green tarp.

For most of July, we sold bread and milk around the neighbourhood. Donny had made a list. Before that first morning we went, he'd gone around to see who wanted to buy from us. Deliveries were made in a pickup truck Donny would borrow from his landscaping job. His boss got free bread. The other landscapers had to pay for whatever they ordered. In the evenings, Donny, Ray and me drove around making the deliveries. While I ran orders up to a house and collected money, they waited in the pickup, getting the next order ready.

The Chinaman lived closest. I walked over with his order. He bought milk. Three bags every few days. Donny told me to give him a pie or doughnuts and not to charge him extra. He told me that when I took it, to call the Chinaman by his real name, to call him *Mr. Lore.* Only Ma called him that. She found out his name after Ray and Gordon spray painted on his fence. One night, they found a can of green spray paint. Before they busted it open to get the marble out, they sprayed *fuck fuck fuck* and *pussyface chink* on the Chinaman's fence. The next day, Ray had paint smeared on his T-shirt. When Ma came home from work, she told us that she saw Mr. Lore in the alley trying to get graffiti off his fence.

"Who?" Ray and me asked.

Ma said, "The Asian man who lives on the other side of the laneway." She had stopped to talk with him. That's how she found out his name. He was using a wire brush and soap and water. It wouldn't come off. I didn't think he spoke English.

After Ray left, Ma asked me what I knew about it. I knew it was Ray and Gordon but I didn't tell her. That same night,

Gordon had sprayed *I hate yur ghuts* on the wall behind Dominion.

There were a lot of stops. Doug Fogal bought a bag of milk and doughnuts. He paid what he could. Donny and him had gone to Eastern Tech together. After high school, he moved to Hamilton for work. A few months later, he went blind from chemicals splashing in his eyes. When he came back to Toronto, he tried to hang himself. Now he's a piano tuner. He lived in the garage behind his sister's place on Woodmount. It never failed, every time I was halfway up the alley with the order, Donny would call me back, reminding me to put the bag of milk *in* Dougie's fridge myself. Before I did, I was to make sure it was plugged in and running.

There was a person in an apartment over a restaurant on the Danforth who wouldn't open his door. After I'd knock, I'd hear stuff being moved around, heavy noises, and then a muffled voice pressed against the door instructing me to leave the bread on the floor in the hall. A two-dollar bill and coins were slid under the door.

Back in the pickup, I gave Donny the money. As he was putting it into an envelope, I asked him how he knew these people.

He shrugged. All he'd tell me was, "I just do."

There were the Farrells, there were the Martins, Travis Hamm's ma, the Rusks, and the Busos. Two of the Busos were albinos, the dad and his boy, Jim. The lane behind their house was called Albino Alley. When I was a kid, if you went down there certain nights, everyone said that's what you'd become.

Halfway through the deliveries, we'd stop at 7-Eleven for Big Gulps. On the curb in the parking lot, Donny would open doughnuts and between sips of Coke, we'd eat and smoke and goof around. Somehow, Ray would work it in that we should be delivering bread and milk to Gordon's family. He said the Daniels shouldn't have to pay for it, either. Donny always said no way, that the Daniels were welfare cases. They could get their own.

Ray pretended it didn't bug him. He shrugged, "At least give 'em doughnuts for the ma."

No matter how much Ray went on, Donny kept telling him, no. After a couple of nights of this, Donny got pissed off. Grabbing Ray by the sleeve, he shoved him against the side of the pickup, snarling, "Will ya stop asking!"

The farthest delivery was Pop-Bottle Tim's. Thursdays and Mondays he bought three breads, a cherry pie, hot dog buns and a bag of 2%.

It was planned that way. Donny's known Pop-Bottle a long time. When he was younger, Donny used to hang out at his house, messing around with his radio equipment. Each spring, Pop-Bottle used to pay Donny and Ray a few bucks to help him deliver telephone books. Even now, if he's got something heavy to take to the scrappers, he'll ask Donny for a hand.

Pop-Bottle lived with his daughter in a neat little semi across Connery Field by the pool. A thirty-foot aerial towered above their house. Neighbours complained it interfered with their TV's reception. It was wired into Pop-Bottle's ham radio. He had a police scanner and could pick up shortwave, too. A bumper sticker on his truck read *VE3 Echo Whiskey Bravo*. Donny told me that was the name Pop-Bottle went by on the ham radio. Except for Donny, nobody called him *Tim*.

All I knew about India was, she was older than me, she was deaf and she had no ma. Because she couldn't hear, she went to a special school. Since seeing her swimming, I've wanted to find out more about her. I could ask Donny but I haven't.

People stay away from Pop-Bottle because he's kind of grubby. After a day of collecting scrap metal or looking for empties, his coveralls are dirty like he's been working under a car. They stay away from India because they think she's a little retarded. She's not. Actually, she's pretty and smart. She reads lips.

By the time we got up to Pop-Bottle's house, it was dark. Him and India were sitting on plastic chairs on their porch facing each other, talking. When her dad looked out to the street and waved to us, India looked at him and then looked at what he was looking at. Turning, she brushed strands of loose hair off her face, tucking them behind her ear. At first, she didn't recognize the pickup. When she did, she gave a little wave. Sitting between Donny and Ray, I felt my face go red and my ears get warm. I was glad it was dark. Donny and Ray didn't notice.

Donny parked and turned the engine off. When we got out, he reached into the back and lifted Tim's order out. Shoving the cardboard box into my arms, Donny said, "Here. Take it." Ray and me followed him up onto the porch.

The porch light was bright. Moths and June bugs buzzed around the bulb. Crickets peeped. With a pair of wire strippers, Pop-Bottle had been peeling the plastic casing off thin lengths of copper wire. Bits of plastic littered the porch boards around his boots, scattered about like pieces of red and black licorice. By his knee, burnished wire spilled over the rim of a metal bucket.

Holding the box of bread close to my chest, I looked at the cherry pie on top. When I said *Hi*, I didn't look up. Pop-Bottle took the box into the house. He came back with beers and set them on a wooden spool he'd turned on its side to use as a table. Removing an opener from a pocket in his coveralls, he popped the caps off and handed the first bottle to India. As he did, he asked her if she wouldn't mind getting three more chairs from the backyard.

Before she could answer, Donny told her, "Mike'll help ya."

Nodding, I followed her back between the houses, listening to her flip-flops slap against her heels. In my head, I could see her submerged, pushing off from the side of the pool, her body stone smooth, slicing the water.

It was dark. There was a gate. It was closed. I didn't expect her to stop so suddenly. I bumped her shoulder. Turning my head instinctively, my cheek brushed against her hair. I felt stupid. I mumbled, "Sorry."

Back on the porch, Ray lit a cigarette. Smoke coiled around his head. He offered the pack to India. "Want one?"

She shook her head, smiled. "No. Thank you. I don't smoke." Her teeth were white and straight.

Ray offered Pop-Bottle a cigarette. Running his fingers through his short cropped hair, he looked at the cigarettes like he wanted one but shook his head, "I'm tryin' to quit." At that, Donny told Ray to put them back in his jacket and to butt out the one he'd lit. Pop-Bottle told Ray he didn't have to. He went inside to get an ashtray. While he was inside, Donny told Ray, when that one's smoked, don't light another one.

Donny and Pop-Bottle and Ray talked. India didn't say much except when Donny asked her what she was doing for the summer. She told us about her job as a lifeguard at a day-camp for deaf kids. As she told us about her job, I wondered how she learned to talk. For a deaf person, her voice sounded pretty normal.

Pop-Bottle asked Donny about Ma. "She's good," he replied. Pop-Bottle asked me if I had a summer job. I told him about working at the Ex in August.

For the rest of the time, I just listened and sipped beer. By the time my first bottle was empty, it had got warm and was nearly flat. I peeled the label off. Pop-Bottle brought out more. Glancing at India when I thought she wouldn't notice, I imagined what it would be like not to hear. It must be like being alone all the time, or being underwater, forever. Except for deaf people on the subway who want money for those sign-language cards they hand you, India was the only deaf person I'd ever seen. I wondered if they were all as quiet as she was.

India's toenails were painted red. Around her ankle, she had a few mosquito bites. Her legs were tanned. They looked so smooth. The shape of her vaccination scar on her bare shoulder reminded me of a crescent moon turned on its side, or maybe a droplet of water. Resting the beer bottle between her legs on the lawn chair, she clasped the top of the bottle and absentmindedly circled the rim with her thumb. Even though she didn't speak, she watched Donny and Ray and her dad's conversation as though she was a part of it. When Ray spoke with an unlit cigarette parked in the corner of his mouth, India tilted her head, puzzled.

Every so often, I'd get a whiff of chlorine. India caught me looking across at the pool. She smiled. Tilting her head back, she brought her bottle to her lips. Her Adam's apple rose and plunged as she drank. As she was taking the last swallow, I looked back at the pool.

India stood. She said she was going inside. Pop-Bottle looked directly at her. He said, "When you go in could you turn off the porch light, please?"

Grinning, Donny and Ray and me nodded. Donny said, "Seeya, India."

Ray muttered, "Yeah. Seeya."

I crossed my legs. I uncrossed them. Crossed them again. I wanted to say more then just *Seeya*. "'Night," was the only thing I could think of.

She eased the screen door closed and the porch went dark. With the porch light off, it was hard to see. Wherever I looked, yellow-white blotches flashed in my vision. As my sight adjusted, Pop-Bottle apologized, telling us how it was difficult for India to follow a conversation if too many people were speaking.

Donny and Ray nodded slowly, thinking they'd done something wrong, maybe hurt India's feelings. It was quiet a minute. A few houses over, an air conditioner kicked on. Hesitantly, Donny said, "That's not why she went inside was it, Tim?"

"No, no, that's not why. Probably just tired. She worked today."

Ray started saying something stupid about how if India wanted, she could come back out and we'd take turns talking.

Pop-Bottle interrupted him. Waving his hand toward Ray, Pop-Bottle said, "No. No, Ray, it's not like that." So Ray wouldn't feel bad, he joked, "And Donny, will ya let your brother light that goddamn cigarette before I take it from him and smoke it myself?"

Ray laughed until he started coughing. Donny chuckled. Instead of telling Ray it was okay to smoke, he gave a quick nod that meant, go ahead. A match flared and a soft orange glow lit up Ray's face.

We stayed a bit longer. Pop-Bottle got more beers. Donny went inside with him. While they talked in the kitchen, Ray took a piss in the bushes beside the porch. Through the window, I could see in the living room, the dining room and some of the kitchen. Their house was neat. It didn't look cluttered. In a corner of the living room, there was a table with radio equipment set up on it. India wasn't around. She must've gone upstairs. Ray came back up on the porch and lit a smoke. Donny and Pop-Bottle came back outside. I pretended to be looking at something near the sidewalk. I didn't want another beer but Pop-Bottle offered me one and I took it anyway. Taking small sips, I glanced inside the house when I didn't think I'd be noticed.

I didn't see India until we were leaving. Ray and Donny were ahead of me, getting into the pickup when the porch light came back on. I heard the front door open. India called through the screen, "Mike. Wait."

Until then, I hadn't noticed the crickets had gone quiet. My face was hot. Somewhere along the street another air conditioner came on. I glanced at my shoes, the path, then at Donny and Ray in the truck. The screen door squeaked. I turned. India had stepped out onto the porch in her bare feet.

"Here." India came down the steps. She had a dog's leash in her hand. I didn't take it. I kept my face down.

"You left it at the pool. You guys have a dog?"

"Yeah. No. Umm, well we sort've, not— It's for—"

Placing a finger at my chin, she gently raised my face. "I can't see what you're saying. To read your lips, Mike, I need your mouth."

"Oh yeah, sorry." I reached for the leash to take it, but she did not let it go.

"Come by tomorrow," she said, "I'm off."

Looking over my shoulder, Donny and Ray sat in the pickup, smoking. Each time they took a drag, their cigarettes brightened.

I heard Ray say, "Come on. What's he doin'. Let's go."

Donny told him, "Wait."

I wanted to tell India, *okay*, but it wouldn't come out.

Like she knew what I was thinking, she let the leash go and she said, "Just tell your brothers you're checking out my dad's ham radio."

She didn't wait for my answer. By the time I said, "Okay," she was nearly inside. I stood holding the leash, wrapping it around my hand, staring up at the house, expecting the porch light to turn off. It didn't.

Until my job at the Ex started, on her days off and on weekends, I spent a lot of time with India. The first time I went to her house without Donny and Ray, I felt like an idiot. I was glad Pop-Bottle's truck wasn't parked at the front of their house. I didn't feel like explaining why I was there.

The porch had been swept. The empty beer bottles were gone. Those chairs me and India had brought from the backyard had been put back. The ashtray Ray used was still sitting on the spool table, but it had been cleaned. Along the windowsill there were flowers in clay pots. They were all different colours but mostly purple. The night before, I'd never noticed them.

As I pressed the doorbell, I wondered, if India's deaf, how's she going to hear it? Maybe it would be better if Pop-Bottle *was* home, then I wouldn't have to stand here like a goof pressing the door-bell for nothing. Taking my finger off the button, I figured it would be better if he *wasn't* home, that way Donny and Ray wouldn't find out I'd been here. But say India got called in this morning to fill in for a lifeguard who didn't show up for work and only Pop-Bottle *was* home? What excuse would I give him? Say nobody's home? What was I doing here? Maybe I should knock. Maybe I should just leave. Clenching my hands, I exhaled and tried to relax. I opened the screen door and knocked. After I knocked a long time, I decided to go home. Halfway down the steps, the door opened.

Pop-Bottle stood in the doorway, a blue laundry basket filled with folded clothing under his arm. He was wearing a clean white T-shirt and jeans. This was the first time I'd ever seen Pop-Bottle not wearing coveralls.

By the way he said, "Hey, Mike," it sounded like he wasn't surprised to see me. I went back up onto the porch, thinking quick about what to say next.

Before I could speak Pop-Bottle said, "Hope you weren't out here long. I was in the basement folding laundry, then I threw in another load. Ya should've rung the doorbell."

"I did but, umm, I didn't think— It must be broke."

Coming out on the porch in his bare feet, Pop-Bottle tried the bell. No chime sounded. I sighed. "See. It don't work."

"Ya, it does." He pressed it a second time, pointing with his chin toward a dim light bulb flashing above the hall closet. "The whole house is wired for India. Phone works the same way, too."

"Oh. Really? How's she ta—" I stopped. I looked at my shoes.

"So, what's up Mike, what can I do for you?"

I wasn't sure what to say. I said *umm* a few times. Pop-Bottle stepped back inside. He wiped his feet on a carpet.

"I was, umm, wondering, remember how Donny used to, umm, when he was younger, you used to let him mess around with your radios? I was thinking, could I check them out? 'Cause— 'cause I'm thinking about getting one," I lied.

He shook his head and chuckled the same way Donny did. "Yeah, sure, Mike. Come on in."

Their house smelled like pine, like real Christmas trees. Expecting to follow him in the living room where the radios were, I wasn't sure where to go when he started up the stairs.

"Hold on," he told me. Grinning, he winked, "I was just messin' with you, Mike. India told me last night you'd be comin' over. I'll go tell her you're here."

Without moving too far from the front door, I looked around their house. Except for the black and white tiles at the entrance and down the hallway, most of the floor, even in the kitchen, was dark hardwood. Where there was carpet, none of it was stained. Framed photographs of people taken a long time ago hung on the walls. I stepped into the living room a little. The cushions on the chesterfield matched. There were bookshelves.

On the top of a bookshelf, in a frame made of glass, was a photograph of a family. I could tell the frame had been repaired by the way glue had oozed out of the cracks when it was drying. Probably been dropped or knocked over. The photo showed a man and a lady and a girl. The girl had big freckles all over her face. The man was holding the little girl's hand. It looked like Pop-Bottle, only younger. The lady was pretty. It was taken at the Riverdale Zoo. It was in colour. They were all smiling, but the man smiled the most.

I walked a little more into the living room. I liked how their house was so clean. Maybe I should've taken my shoes off. Even the table the radio equipment was on was neat. They didn't look like normal radios. These ones were more like transmitters and receivers. They had dials and switches and gauges. There was a thing like a CB microphone. Instead of holding it in your hand and pressing a button on the side to talk, this one was about eight inches high. It had a square green button at the base.

Certificates that looked like licences were mounted on the wall. A black and white photograph, nearly as big as a poster, was taped up beside them. It showed a man with a moustache wearing an old-fashioned hat. Standing outside a castle in the middle of nowhere, he's looking directly into the camera. The picture was taken on a windy day. Antennas stick out of the top of the castle. The man looked Italian or maybe Greek. It's hard to tell because it was taken so long ago. In the bottom right-hand corner, someone had written *Marconi at Signal Hill 1901*. I wondered who Marconi was. By the way he was dressed, in suit with a striped vest, he looked important. In those days though, everyone looked important. I knew he couldn't be related to Pop-Bottle because Pop-Bottle was born around here.

Other things were taped to the wall. A chart showing Morse code. From *A* to *Z,* there followed letters and dots and dashes. Printed on another sheet was something called *The International Phonetic Alphabet.* It made more sense than Morse code. I began reading softly, "*A*-Alpha, *B*-Bravo, *C*-Charlie,—" When I got to *G*-golf, India and her dad came into the living room.

Pop-Bottle must've heard me. He told me to keep going, "Don't stop. Keep reading it out."

I felt dumb. India smiled. She wore her hair in a ponytail. I smiled back. I noticed she had little freckles on her cheeks. I continued reading, "*H*-Hotel, *I*-India?" I stopped.

"Keep going."

J-Juliet, *K*-kilo, *L*-Lima, *M*-Mike, *N*-Novemb—"

Pop-Bottle interrupted, "Stop. A funny coincidence, eh?"

I asked, "What is?"

"Both *Mike* and *India* are in the phonetic alphabet."

India rolled her eyes. "Dad—" she sighed, gently nudging him, "that would also be true if Mike was named *Oscar.*" They both laughed.

I didn't get it. I wasn't sure if they were making fun of me until I read farther down and came to O. "*O*-Oscar," I said. I imagined what it would be like being called *Oscar* all my life.

Smirking, Pop-Bottle added, "Or Romeo." He winked. I scanned down to R. Romeo.

"Or Zulu." India cut in.

They both laughed. I didn't until I got to *Z*-Zulu. I felt like joking, *That would be the name of a black person.* I wasn't sure if they'd think that was funny, so I kept it to myself.

India told her dad that we were going out, that she'd be home around dinner.

Pop-Bottle said, "Okay." He shook my hand. "Good to see you again, Mike. Say hello to your mother. And to Donny and Ray."

"I will."

India was already at the door, "Come on Mike, let's go." I followed her onto the porch.

When India didn't have to work, we went out places. Not to movies or places like that. Some days we'd just sit across the road in Connery Park by the pool. On the other side of the fence, kids chased one another, dove, splashed. Lifeguards continuously blowing their whistles, barking warnings about running, about diving in the shallow end.

One evening, a men's league was playing softball at the diamond. In the half-filled stands, we watched until the game was rained out. Everyone ran for cover except us. The dugout emptied. Both teams left. From beneath the dugout's overhang, we watched the storm. It poured. Lightning jabbed from cloud to cloud, down to the ground. When it thundered, India said she could feel it in her feet and up into her chest. We only got a little wet.

Another time, we took a bus and a streetcar down to the lake, to the boardwalk at Kew Beach. Jingling bells attached to handlebars, the Dickie-Dee man stood beside his white icebox bicycle, a crowd pressing in around him. Waiting our turn, we bought Fudgesicles and ate them on the bleachers around the Olympic Pool.

Sitting so close our legs touched, we watched swimmers in colourful bathing suits climb the rungs of the highest diving platform, fifteen metres up. Convincing themselves they could, in blinding sunlight, they'd inch reluctantly to the edge, then, arms way up high, a few quick breaths, head tucked tight against their chest, they'd jump. Toppling forward, somehow converting a fall into a dive, like a needle, they speared the water's surface. Then just as quick, they'd shoot back up, reemerging, gasping the air.

India asked, "Would you do that?"

I knew I never would. Instead of answering right away, I chewed on my Fudgesicle stick, pretending to be thinking it over. After a minute, I told her, "It depends. Would you?"

She didn't reply. She couldn't understand what I'd said. She took the Fudgesicle stick out of my mouth "Pardon?"

I wanted to lie. I was honest, though. "No. It's way too high. Would you?"

"I already have."

On a Sunday morning, we took the ferry to Ward's Island. Wandering the paths, we stayed there all day. India brought sandwiches wrapped in wax paper. I brought two bruised apples and a pack of honey-glazed doughnuts. Leaning on the rail of a wooden bridge that arched across a lagoon, we stopped to eat. Between bites, we pinched small pieces of the bread and flicked them to the ducks and geese that swam in the stagnant water below. Not far away, on the grass, a couple threw a frisbee to one another. In a barbeque pit, a man was cooking wieners and hamburgers for his family. Swallowed up in clouds of smoke, his wife yelled at him, he was burning their lunch.

India told me about being deaf. I asked if she was born that way.

"I could hear until I was eight. Then I got chicken pox."

"You went deaf from chicken pox?"

"It's rare, but it happens."

"You can't hear nothing?"

She brushed crumbs off her hands. "Just a tiny bit. It's not as bad as you think, Mike. When you go deaf, you learn to *see* sounds, *see* what people are saying."

"Like lip reading?"

"Reading lips is part of it. But I also learned to *hear* by seeing how a person stands, how they move their hands, the changes in their face. All of those things. People don't realize how loud they speak with their eyes. Even eyebrows tell me stuff. As they talk, I watch the way muscles in the neck move. Details show me what they're saying."

The planks on the bridge vibrated as a boy on a bicycle rode past. A second boy followed, chasing him on foot.

I said, "That must be hard."

"It is if too many people talk at once or if they chew gum or have something in their mouth like a pencil or a cigarette. But a lot of times, I think I hear more by *seeing*. By watching, people tell me things they don't mean to. The difference between you and me, Mike, I had to learn to *see* voices, while you've always just heard them."

I didn't get it. I put my hands in my pockets. "How can you *see* voices?"

"A lot comes from the *seeing* I hear in my head. Some voices and sounds are from memory. Imagine a bell, you remember what it looks like and you hear it ring without even trying. Voices are the same. I *see* my dad's voice from back when I could hear." She paused, scratching her shoulder and then said, "You try it. Think of your mom's voice. Remember something she said today or yesterday."

I could see Ma in my head. I could hear her voice. I grinned.

"See," India said, "that's *seeing* a voice."

Sort of understanding what she was talking about, I nodded, "Oh, yeah."

India could tell I didn't really get it. Tucking a strand of hair behind her ear, she explained, "Think about this, Mike. People who have their leg amputated or a hand cut off swear years later they can still feel tingling in their fingers. It's a phantom sensation. The fingers aren't there anymore. I see sounds, voices in particular, like that." She pointed at a duck, paddling in a circle, its webbed feet stirring up sediment in the shallow black water. Because we'd stopped feeding them, the other ducks had swum away. Hoping for more crumbs, the lone duck quacked. At the far end of the lagoon, the other ducks and geese answered, quacking and ruffling their wings.

India told me, "I can't hear that now at all, Mike, but I see you look across the lagoon. I see where you look. I see the ducks with their beaks opening and closing. I see and I remember the sound they make."

India imitated a cat meowing.

I wasn't expecting that. I made a funny face.

India laughed. Putting her arm over my shoulder, she pulled me closer to her and made the sound of a duck quacking. "I was just seeing if you were paying attention."

I laughed.

"Being deaf makes me observant. You're sort of the same way, Mike. You're doing it all the time. I've seen you watching, remembering."

"What? I do?"

"Yes. Like that first morning at the pool. I watched you. I saw you from the water. The way you were looking all around the park, I could see you *remembering*."

I thought back to that morning. It seemed so long ago. Waiting for Donny and Ray, thinking about Ma and the fireworks. About climbing the tree to watch India underwater.

We left the bridge and walked to the lake. I reached for India's hand and held it. On a bench by the shore, we sat close, looking back across the bay, bank towers, the expressway, hotels, Union Station, the entire city reflected in the shimmering face of the bay.

"India?"

"Yes."

"Umm, what's my voice look like?"

She thought a long time before answering, "Your voice is soft. No sharp edges."

Straightening, I wasn't expecting this. "What about Donny's? What about Ray's?"

"Donny's voice is blunt. It is a stick snapping. Ray speaks with his shoulders or doesn't speak at all. Mostly, his voice is a shrug."

I wasn't sure if this was bad or good so I didn't ask any more questions.

Low behind buildings in the west, the sun was giant and orange. We looked directly into it without squinting. Before our eyes, evening arrived, bringing with it hardly any stars. Across the water, we saw one city go to sleep and another awake beneath a glowing blanket of night.

A few days later, I stayed late at India's house. Pop-Bottle was home, inside, talking on the ham radio. In the backyard, with the outside light on, India and me played cards. She taught me Crazy Eights. Pop-Bottle came out and lit mosquito coils. He brought out sliced watermelon on a plate and set it on the picnic table. It was raining but we were under a canopy. India asked her dad if he wanted to play. He did.

The rain had stopped a long time before I was leaving. Pop-Bottle offered to drive me home. I told him, no thanks. India walked with me to the sidewalk. Together, we walked a little until we were standing under a streetlamp a few houses down. The road was wet, puddles reflecting streetlights and porch lights. Everything smelled like rain, like grass.

Saying goodbye felt different tonight. I wasn't sure how to do it. Looking all around, I said, "Umm, maybe I'll see you tomorrow?"

At first, whenever I was with India, I had to remind myself to look at her when I'd speak. If I didn't, she'd place a finger under my chin and raise my face.

"That's a habit," she had told me. "You look down a lot when you talk."

"I do?"

She'd said it wasn't just with her, either. She noticed I talked that way with almost everyone. Maybe she was right.

After she told me that, when I thought no one was looking, I practiced walking with my head up. Ma asked me if I'd hurt my neck. I'd try reading my own lips. It wasn't easy. One time, Ray caught me in the kitchen mouthing, *hell-o*, *hell-o* at my reflection in the toaster.

He'd scoffed, "Hey Donny, check it out, Mikey's talkin' to the toaster."

So I wouldn't look stupid, I pretended to pick at something stuck in my teeth. I said, "No, I ain't. A sesame seed's stuck in my tooth."

Pop-Bottle came out onto the porch and looked up and down the street. Before he could see us, India pulled me by the arm out from under the streetlight. We stood between two parked cars. I looked at my shoes. I quickly looked back up again. India put her finger under my chin anyway, guiding her mouth to mine. Her lips were sweet like strawberry. As though delicately passing a slippery watermelon seed between us, our tongues touched softly.

By the time I'd walked home, it was about three. Two hours later Donny shook me awake to go for bread. Ray was already out in the van. My eyes wouldn't open. Donny let me sleep. Before leaving, he knelt beside the bed, whispering forcefully, "Tonight you gotta still come to make the deliveries."

We stopped taking milk. I came up the back alley one afternoon and found Donny hauling away the fridge. Where it had been sitting up against the house, there was a square patch of yellowed grass. Mice had been living under it. In one corner, there was a flattened nest made of dryer lint, chewed plastic the same colour as the tarp, cherry pits and seeds. The fridge was already loaded into the landscaping truck. Donny had done it himself. Ray was out with Gordon.

"Hey, Mike." He wound the length of an extension cord from his elbow and his thumb. "How's India?"

"Good. Fridge broke?"

Donny hung the extension cord from a nail driven into the mortar between the bricks. "No. See Tim?"

"Yeah. Why you takin' it?"

Picking up the folded tarps, he walked to the truck. "Don't need it no more." Donny tried to shove the fridge, checking to see if it was secure. He'd slid it in on its side. It didn't budge. He said, "Ya know, when I was a kid, I used to pretend India was my little sister."

"Really?" I couldn't imagine Donny pretending anything.

"Yeah. When she went deaf, her ma took it hard. 'Cause of how she acted after that, when they found her dead, people said she'd done it to herself. It wasn't true. She didn't mean to do it, but it don't matter 'cause people talked anyways." Donny rubbed his chin, "Tim got a ton of cash from the insurance. You think they would've paid if it was a suicide?"

"Where'd they find her?"

Donny closed the tailgate. "In the tub. She was havin' a bath or something. Took too many pills by mistake. Passed out. Slipped under water. Drowned." The way he looked around, it was like he was remembering the whole thing. He sighed. "Tim told me when India found her, she got in the tub beside her ma, pulled the plug and then just sat there wet."

I'd never heard any of this before.

Donny got into the truck. The key was in the ignition already. He turned it. The engine hesitated before starting. He said, "Won't be doin' the milk no more, Mike—"

He said something else, something about Ray and him and me going to the Ex to get ID and our pictures taken. I wasn't really listening. I was thinking about India finding her ma drowned in their bathtub, wondering, wasn't a tub too small for drowning in?

I was glad we weren't doing the milk no more. I didn't want to go for bread. I didn't want to make the deliveries. I was tired of it. The money wasn't even so good. I should've told Donny right then, before he pulled away, but I didn't.

By the first week of August, the sun was coming up about an hour later. All the time, I was yawning and stretching and rubbing my eyes. The days India worked, I slept. A few times, I'd just be getting up when Ma would be coming in from work. Standing in the bedroom doorway, she asked if I was okay. She said lately I'd been looking tired.

Ray called out from the kitchen, "He's fine, he's just in love."

Turning her head, Ma called back, "What?"

"He can't get enough of India."

Sitting up, I ran my hands through my hair.

Ma said, "Who?"

The parking lot at the 7-Eleven was bright, lit by the store's greenish-orange fluorescent sign. Garbage overflowed from the concrete trashcans. Chocolate bar wrappers, flattened coffee cups, crushed pop cans and discarded lottery tickets littered the ground around them. Every so often, someone would park beside us. Leaving the engine idling, they'd hop out of their car, run into the store, buy what they needed, hurry out and quickly pull away.

Besides Donny and Ray and me, only the taxi drivers stuck around. Waiting on a call from dispatch or taking a break from driving fares, cabbies read newspapers, folded and torn, or talked in their own language with other drivers who'd parked their cab side by side but facing the opposite direction.

Standing beside the pickup with his arms folded across his chest, Donny told Ray and me that once the Ex opened, we were done selling bread. The last two times we'd been out delivering, we hadn't sold milk. He said we'd go to Dominion only one more morning.

Earlier that day, Donny took off from his landscaping job and met Ray and me at Bathurst station. The three of us took the 511 streetcar into the Exhibition grounds. It was crowded. The Ex ran for three weeks, closing on Labour Day. They needed lots of workers. The lineups for getting your picture taken were long. Before waiting in that line, we had to get in another one where they told us the specific jobs we'd been hired to do. The jobs Donny and Ray got were way better than mine. Ray would work on the Midway at a game. Donny was in maintenance. I'd be getting paid to walk around with a bag and broom sweeping garbage up off the ground.

I sat on the curb sipping Coke through a straw. The parking lot reeked of car exhaust. Other times I liked the smell, but tonight, it was giving me a headache. I wished we'd go home. There were still two more places left to drop off bread. It was about ten or ten-thirty. I was tired. The night before, I had been over at India's until late. We messed around in her bedroom until two in the morning. If Ray hadn't woke me to go to the Ex, I'd have slept until Ma came home

Glancing all around the parking lot, Donny unfolded his arms. I stood and stretched. Yawning, I handed the Big Gulp to Donny. He took a sip and handed it back. Offering the Coke to Ray, he shook his head, no. Leaning against the side of the pick-up, Ray took a drag off his cigarette. He stuffed little white dough-nuts into his mouth. He'd eaten nearly the whole pack himself. The icing sugar around his mouth made him look like a clown putting makeup on.

Donny said, "I started telling people we wouldn't be selling the bread anymore."

Ray swallowed hard. Smoke streaming from his nose and mouth, he said, "Who? Who'd ya tell?"

"What difference does it make?"

"Just tell me. Who'd ya tell so far?"

Donny rhymed off names, "Told Travis Hamm's ma. Told Mr. Rusk. Tim. The Farrells—"

Pointing at himself, then at Donny and me, Ray's voice cracked, "Why ya gotta tell 'em? If *we're* not gunna do it, Gordie and me can take it over."

Raising his voice, Donny said firmly, "Once we stop, no one else takes it over, especially not you and Buttfuck."

Donny's voice got the attention of a cab driver parked close by.

"Mike wants to keep sellin' bread, don't ya, Mike?"

Balancing the Big Gulp on the side of the pickup, before I could say *no, not really*, Donny cut in. Even louder, he snarled,

"How? Youse got no truck. Youse can't get waybills. And between you and that idiot Gordon, ya both got no brains."

Usually when Donny got hot like this, Ray would shrug it off and back down right away. This time, he wouldn't let it go. "Me and Gordie and Mike could do it easy, eh Mike?"

Looking at my shoes, at the numerous blots of bubblegum, black and flattened into the asphalt like coins, I mumbled, "Nah, I don't think so."

Even though it was Donny he was pissed with, Ray went off on me. "That's 'cause all you want to do is fuck around with India all the time—"

Taking a quick step toward Ray, through clenched teeth Donny snapped, "Shut your fuckin' mouth, Ray, she ain't got nothin' to do with it."

"Yeah, she does. If Mikey wasn't—"

Donny didn't let him finish. Taking Ray by the arm, he shook him hard. "Listen Ray, we're not doin' the bread thing no more. It's finished. No one's doin' it. Not you. Not Mikey and not Butt-fuck. No way. You know how lucky we've been? Haven't seen the cops *one* fuckin' morning." Donny raised his index finger putting it right in Ray's face. Ray tried to turn away but Donny held it there in front of him. "Know why? I'll tell you why. They change up their shifts. *Night* goes off at six-thirty, *day* comes on. But for an hour or so before that, cops park their cruisers behind a factory or down a dead-end street where they won't be seen, and then doze away the time, waitin' for their twelve hours to be done."

Donny stepped back. He looked around. All the taxi drivers had stopped reading their newspaper and talking to see what was getting him so loud.

Ray took a crushed pack of cigarettes out of his shirt pocket. Only half the pack had been smoked. He put one in his mouth but didn't light it. It hung there, loose between his lips. Ray did not offer one to Donny or me. Donny grabbed the pack anyway and took one, tucking it behind his ear for later. Throwing the cigarette pack in through the driver's side window, Donny put his hand on the door handle and told us, "Come on, let's go."

Ray padded his pockets for his lighter. He shrugged, "So what —Big deal. Everyone knows about cops sleeping in their cruisers."

Turning, Donny squinted "So what? Big deal? Would you or Buttfuck have bothered to figure out when they change shifts? Eh? Would ya?"

Ray didn't answer. With the unlit cigarette hanging off his bottom lip, Ray scoffed, "So if we didn't have to worry about cops why'd Mikey have to come?"

Ray had a point. Glancing at me quick, all Donny answered was, "'Cause."

"'Cause why?"

"I just told you." Donny moved close to Ray, jabbing his finger hard into the centre of Ray's chest. "Just 'cause."

Ray smirked, "You were just tryin' to hook him up with India. You and Pop-Bottle both. Youse knew Mikey'd see 'er at the pool. Every-one knows about her pool-hopping. Gordie watches 'er all the time. Fuckin' guy sits up a tree on the other side of the fence like a monkey jacking off the whole time." As Ray chuckled, the unlit cigarette jerked up and down between his lips.

Donny shook his head. Under his breath, he called Gordon a fucking pig.

Ray kept going, "Yeah, but you know what's really fuckin' gross? Check out this. Gordie told me people up around where they live say Pop-Bottle's banging his daughter." Throwing his head back, he closed his eyes and laughed.

In a second, Donny and me were on Ray. Donny got him first, pushing him hard against the side of the truck. The Big Gulp fell to the ground. Coke spilled everywhere. Donny's hand came up fast, clamping around Ray's throat like a vice. Ray's eyes bulged. He looked terrified. From the side, I cracked Ray in the mouth, crushing the unlit cigarette into his face. His expression changed from frightened to confused.

Donny's fingers tightened around Ray's windpipe. I tried to get another shot in but Donny turned Ray so I couldn't. Ray was changing colour. For saying that about India, just for a second, I wanted Donny to not stop strangling him.

Bits of tobacco stuck to his face. His lip was bleeding. Close up in Ray's face, Donny calmly spit out, "Don't ever say that again. Ever."

A car pulled into the spot beside us. A man got out. He went into the 7-Eleven.

Donny let Ray go. Ray doubled-over, coughing, spitting. With the back of his hand, he wiped his mouth. There was blood. Already, his lip was swelling.

None of us spoke. Between the icing sugar, the blood and the brown flecks of tobacco, Ray's face was a mess.

Donny told him to wipe it off, but Ray ignored him. He told him again, "Wipe your face off, Ray. Use your shirt."

Catching me off guard, Ray charged headfirst at me, his shoulder driving into my stomach. I went backward. We both fell on to the ground. The wind was knocked out of me. Ray got his knee up, pressing down on my chest. Instinctively, with one arm protecting my face, I thrust my other hand upward. Only once did it connect with Ray. I nailed him straight up under his jaw, knocking his mouth closed so hard his teeth snapped together with a *clack*.

Right then, he could've beaten the shit out of me. He had me
pinned. Not one of his punches landed, though. It was more like he
was throwing his hands at me, cuffing and slapping. Donny placed
a hand on Ray's shoulder, yanking him off. Behind us, in the store
window, a Philipino cashier and a man wearing a tie and a name tag
stood watching us without any expression on their faces.

Ray leaned against the truck, rubbing his jaw and panting.
Donny stood between us looking down at me. Sitting on the curb,
I gasped, trying to catch my breath. Somewhere in the parking lot,
car brakes squeaked. I figured it was a taxi until a white, scuffed
bumper inched into view around the front of the pickup. Glancing
through Donny's legs, I saw a white fender, red and blue strips, the
word POLICE.

The cruiser squeaked to a stop. The window was rolled down.
His wrist draped over the steering wheel, sitting low in the seat, the
officer stared at us.

Ray straightened. Grinning, he gave his face a quick wipe.
Donny had turned and was already moving toward the door of the
cruiser. Before he could get close, Ray stepped in front of him. His
hand at his side, fingers splayed, out of the corner of his mouth, Ray
said fast, "Don, stop. I'll talk."

The cop had a big, flat face darkened with stubble. His eyes
darted, sharp, alert. Above the drone of the engine, he said, "Hey
boys. Everything okay tonight?"

Donny's fingers twitched. One hand curled into a fist. He
rocked a little, like he had something planned, like he was about to
pounce.

Before anything could happen, Ray moved toward the cruiser.
Faking a laugh, he chuckled, "We're just goofing around officer. My
little brother here's acting like he's a big *man*." Without turning,
Ray pointed back at me with his thumb. "You know how it is, eh?"

The officer didn't respond. Instead, he leaned forward, looking past Ray, past Donny. Jabbing his chin at me, he asked, "You okay, son?"

Struggling to control my breathing, I cocked my mouth into a crooked grin, "Yeah."

The whole time he was sizing us up, his partner stared ahead, never bothering to look at us. The officer sighed, "You boys drinking or smoking anything this evening?"

"No, sir. Just cigarettes," Ray said, picking a piece of tobacco off his cheek.

The officer nodded. He looked at us a second longer, scratching his chin. Lifting his foot off the brake pedal, the worn pads squeaking, the cruiser slowly rolled forward.

The cop nodded. We nodded back. The cruiser pulled away.

The man who'd parked beside us came out of the store carrying a bag of milk and a magazine. He got into his car and left.

A couple of minutes later, Donny and Ray and me got in the truck. All the way home, we sat stiff, not talking or moving at all. We'd never had a fight like that before. We didn't do the last deliveries. Ray touched his mouth a lot. He rubbed his bottom lip. At a red light, Donny reached under the seat and pulled out a rag. Without saying anything, he passed it to Ray.

In the laneway behind the house, Ray dug the flattened cigarette pack out from underneath him and asked, "Youse wanna smoke?"

Instead of going in, we smoked crushed cigarettes in the pickup truck. From here, we could see Ma's bedroom. The light was on.

One of my shoes was wet from when the Big Gulp spilt. Wiggling my toes, I looked down at the floorboards. Coke had soaked through my sock.

Donny said, "Ma's gonna ask what happened to your mouth."

Ray told him, "I'll tell 'er Gordie elbowed me by accident."

I wanted to say sorry to Ray but I didn't know how. Instead, I went, "Hmm."

We smoked until Ma's bedroom light went off. A few minutes later, we went in.

The last time we went to the Dominion was the only time it rained. Donny shook me awake. "Let's go."

The window was open. From my bed, I could hear rainwater trickling through the eaves to the down-pipe at the corner of the house.

Lying there with my eyes open, listening, Donny thought I had gone back to sleep. He shook me again, harder. "Come on, get up."

Wiping sleep out of my eye, I went to the window and pulled back the faded bedsheet we used as a curtain. Ray was in the van already. Donny was behind me, doing something in the dark. I whispered, "It's raining."

He whispered back, "So?"

Clouds hung low in the sky. It was foggy. Drivers had their headlights on. I knelt on the floorboards between Donny and Ray. The van's front window kept fogging up. Donny tried to clear it off by opening the vents but it didn't make a difference. It was raining too hard to roll the windows down. Even opened a crack, the rain blew in.

The fog was low, shrouding the upper stories of apartment buildings. Because of the clouds, it stayed darker, longer. When we got to the Dominion, we hardly waited. The parking lot lights were off. The circulation fans were humming.

"Okay." Donny turned the van around. Before backing to the shipping doors, I slid the van door open and got out. The rain had become a drizzle.

Rolling down his window, Ray tossed something at me. It was the dog leash.

"Eh, don't forget Buddy," he smirked.

I didn't stick around to watch for police. Even if it didn't make any difference, I should have at least waited for Donny and Ray to back the van up and start loading, but I didn't. Spinning the leash around and around, I started toward Connery Pool, never once looking back. Passing the garbage bin, I let the leash go. It flew into the air and landed far away.

By Ventor Avenue, the rain had stopped completely. Porch lights were still on. Through front windows, I could see people in their living rooms and kitchens eating breakfast or watching TV. Stepping off the sidewalk to let a couple pass, even though it was not raining, they walked close together, sharing an umbrella. A skunk waddled across the road, disappearing under a fence and into a garden. To keep his arm dry, the guy who delivered newspapers from the front seat of his Vega had cut a hole in the bottom of a green garbage bag and pulled it up to his shoulder.

I could smell the chlorine from Connery Pool. The pleasant chemical odour, mixed with the warm smell after a night of summertime rain, gave everything a sweet, earthy scent. The horizon in the east has become a lighter grey. I wasn't expecting to see India. I knew she only went swimming on the mornings she worked. Today, she was working but because of the weather, I figured she wouldn't be in the pool. I looked for her anyway. The grass was sopping wet. The ground was soft. Under a tree at the fence, I stood on my toes, trying to see into the water. The water level was unusually high, higher than I'd ever seen it, nearly even with the pool's blue concrete rim. I wondered if it was filled this much on purpose, or if it was because of all the rain.

Smooth as glass and undisturbed, it looked as though you could walk across its surface. Below the dull sky, the bottom of the pool flashed a brilliant turquoise.

I never saw India until she came up at the far end. Only a quick breath, then she turned underwater, starting back. Half a minute later she resurfaced. Spotting me, she waved, directing me to come in. Looking around, I wondered if India climbed the fence or if she knew another way in. I wondered how much longer until Donny and Ray got here. It was hard to tell. Sometimes they'd take a long time, sometimes they'd come quick. When I looked into the pool again, India was under the water, swimming away from me.

As I climbed the chain-link fence, I had to be careful. It was slippery. The toe of my running shoe was too big for the diamond-shaped openings. They kept slipping out. At the top, I swung my leg over and my shoelace got caught. Working it free, I climbed halfway down then jumped. This was the first time in years I'd been on this side of the fence.

India came up for air. Treading water, she waved again for me to come in. She swam back to the shallow end. Poolside, I took my shoes off, my shirt, socks and pants, leaving them in a pile. Without testing the water, I dove in. I swam across to India. She told me not to splash. It made too much noise. We kissed.

Pulling away, she went underwater, swam another length.

Tugging my earlobe, I jerked my head, side to side, trying to shake water out of my ears. It wouldn't come out. I glanced nervously back at the road, watching for the van. My feet just touching the bottom, I lowered myself until only my nose was above water.

India surfaced behind me. She pulled her goggles off. Her hair was sleek, pulled back from her face and darker than when it was dry. She took my wrist and led us to shallower water. Both the air and the water were warm. Still, raised and hard, goose bumps prickled our flesh.

India said softly, "When it rains, the water is nice and warm." With water plugging my ears, I could barely make out what she had said. Wading in front of me, she pressed her bare chest against mine. Somewhere underwater, India had taken off her bathing suit. Reaching behind me, she snapped the elastic waistband on my underwear. She asked, "Why do you still have these on?"

I said, "Somebody might be watching."

"Nobody's watching. Not even Gordon Daniels."

"You know about that?"

"Yes. Your brother came by. He spoke with my Dad."

I wondered if Donny'd said anything else. Anything about us fighting. Like she knew what I was thinking, she added, "He said that maybe we shouldn't see each other so much."

"Really?"

"Yeah, but who cares what your brother thinks, right?"

Before I answered, she brought her lips to mine and we kissed. I pulled my underwear down, working them off with my foot. Skin touching skin, our bodies brushing hard against one another, I placed a hand at the base of her spine, holding her tight. Our hips came together. She kissed around my lips, chin, my Adam's apple. Cupping her breast, I pressed my tongue into the flesh above her collarbone, kissing up and down her neck.

I wasn't thinking anymore, not about Donny or Ray or anything. It was still kind of dark, but if Tim stepped out onto their porch, he could see across into the pool.

Pulling away a bit so India could see my lips, I asked, "Does your Dad know you do this?"

Catching her breath, she drew me close. She said, "Do what?"

"Swim when the pool's not open."

Arms across one another's shoulders, in the buoyancy of water, we turned in a slow circle.

"Yes. He used to say it's not safe. Sometimes he'd check on me from the porch."

I interrupted, "Does he still?"

"Don't worry, Mike. It's okay."

"Why don't you just go swimming when the pool's open?"

India thought for a while. She said, "Before, when my mom was alive, we played a game at home in the tub. I was little. This was before the chicken pox. I'd hold my breath and go underwater. She'd say something, something like a nursery rhyme or lines from a poem she'd memorized.

"To win, I had to guess what she was saying. I remember holding my breath so long, straining to hear, not wanting to come up until I knew. She'd repeat it again and again. Sometimes, I could make it out, other times, not. I'd come up and tell her what I'd heard. Usually, it was wrong. Sort of like that game, *broken telephone*. When I'd tell her what I thought I'd heard, we'd laugh, she'd tease me, then she'd say the correct line out loud."

Quiet a moment remembering, softly, India recited, "For all smooth lips can say, have given their hearts to the play, and who could play it well enough, if deaf and dumb and blind with love?"

I asked, "What's that mean?" She didn't answer.

"I hated it when I couldn't hear what she was saying. I'd tell her, *One more try, Mom, one more try.* Before she could say no, I'd take a breath and dunk my head under."

India paused. Water trickled down the side of her nose. "I like to be here in the pool all alone. Mornings underwater, it's so quiet I can hear my mother's voice."

She didn't say anything else. Moving backward until her back was against the side of the pool, India closed her eyes. Reaching underwater, I raised her thigh up to my side. She lifted her face. As I went inside, her head tilted back farther, she let out a long, climbing moan.

On the other side of the fence, by the road, the van pulled up. My calf muscles tightened.

India didn't have to look, didn't have to open her eyes. She knew. I tried pulling away, but India held me. I could not let them see me naked, but my clothes were in a pile, too far away.

The van's doors opened, closed. In the morning quiet, Ray's voice, high and breaking, and Donny's, too, carried easily across the park. Water was in my ears. I had to get it out. I wasn't hearing right. I couldn't tell what they were saying.

India whispered, "Take a breath," and we went under.

Eyes open, inches from my face, India was a blur. I could make out red lips, freckled cheeks, the tip of her nose. Framing her face, black strands of hair floated, suspended like long, disconnected fingers. Chlorine stung my eyes. We held each other, and except for the *swoosh* of our free hand combing water, I heard nothing. Holding our breath until our lungs burned, finally, we both came up, gasping.

The van was pulling away. Panting, we worked at slowing our breath. We'd never come apart.

PLAYING BASRA

Ma was sitting on the top step sipping tea from the *World's Greatest Mom* cup Ray got her from Goodwill and telling me her idea about Donny, Ray and I doing something together once Donny was home.

"You need money anyways, right Mike? For books and stuff, and you got the summer off, don't you?"

Through the furnace ducts, the car parts, pipes and busted hockey sticks wedged between the joists of the basement ceiling, I could see only Ma's slippers, her shins and knees. A clothesline went from one corner of the basement to the other. Near the middle, it sagged under the weight of drying shirts and towels, some of them touching the concrete floor. By not using the dryer, we saved money.

Before Ma would say something, she'd lean forward so I could hear her better. After Donny got home, when he was ready to, Ma said Ray and me and him could get some sort of business going.

Reading and listening to her at the same time, I told her, "Yeah, sure."

I had gotten up early and went down to the desk in the basement to study for a Major Authors exam. Closing the book I'd been going over, I leaned back and stretched. Major Authors was my last exam. After that, I was done until September.

"Coke might give me hours," I told her.

Leaning forward, she replied, "But you don't know for sure, do you?"

"Okay, okay, I'll talk to Ray about it."

Since getting laid off from Bombardier, Ray had been making money doing odd jobs. Handyman kind of work, like drywalling, painting, a bit of plumbing. He was good at those sorts of things.

Before I started at York University I had been counting on more money from OSAP. I had enrolled in five courses. Ma told me to give her less rent. By then, Donny was living on a base up north. They didn't pay so well, but he still sent Ma some money. A couple of months later, his regiment was deployed. Around the same time, Ray moved out and there was even less money. I got temp work part-time at Coca-Cola and studied whenever I could. It was hard to work and to study. It wasn't like high school. To have more money, Ma took on another half shift. We talked about ways to spend less. We bought powdered milk again. I stopped buying smokes and skipped lunch or just bought a coffee. When I'd see Ray, I'd bum cigarettes from him.

The extra hours Ma was doing were too much for her. I could tell. She looked tired. So she wouldn't have to work as much, I asked my supervisor at Coke to give me the shifts of any guys who didn't show up for theirs. I dropped two courses and got some tuition money back.

Before the basement was set up, I studied at the table in the dining room. The light was shitty. By one or so in the morning, my eyes hurt from reading and I'd start to doze off. I'd get up and walk around and stretch or make a coffee. If I had a cigarette, I'd go out back for a smoke. The fresh air woke me up.

A lot of times I woke up Ma by accident making too much noise. She said she couldn't go into a deep sleep because she was afraid of missing Donny's phone call. When he did call, it was early in the morning. He didn't call too often and he only spoke with Ma when he did. One time after hanging up, Ma asked me why he couldn't call at another time, when it wasn't so early. I reminded her about time zones. "It's around lunchtime where Donny is, Ma."

To help her know the time where Donny's unit was, I found a windup clock and set the time eight hours ahead. I put it beside the telephone. Most of the time I'd forget to wind it. It didn't really matter what time it was though, she always worried about Donny. Ray and me kept telling her she didn't have too, that nothing was going to happen.

For a long time, nothing did, until one night when the phone rang. It was earlier than the time Donny usually called, but I figured it was him, so I stayed in bed and let Ma get up and answer it. It wasn't Donny. It was a man from the Department of National Defence. I heard Ma gasp. She dropped the receiver onto the cracked linoleum floor. I sat up and turned on the lamp beside the bed. Ma came to my room and stood in the doorway, covering her mouth with both hands. She was shaking. She made a sound like an animal moaning. Donny was dead, I just knew it.

"What! What!"

Ma couldn't speak at all. She followed me back to the dark kitchen. I knelt and picked up the receiver. Putting her hands on my shoulder, Ma stood right beside me, her head dropped against her chest. Crying, she bit her bottom lip as tears soaked my T-shirt.

"Hello?" I told the person on the phone who I was. The DND man did the rest of the talking. The line was bad. In the background, I heard a machine humming. It sounded like a generator. I heard other voices, sharp, urgent. He told me what happened. He said that Donny had been taken.

"We've got boots on the ground as we speak," he said. "The situation is being monitored with extreme circumspection."

Before he hung up, he told me, "Sit tight. And don't watch the news."

A few days after that, I put the windup clock away in the junk drawer. The time where Donny was didn't matter anymore. They couldn't even say for sure in what country he was being held in. His picture was on the front of the newspapers. DND people came to the house. They said if we needed anything, ask. They stressed that progress was being made, that the news reports were inaccurate. When reporters came to the door, we didn't answer it.

When Ray and I talked about Donny, we'd tell each other things we knew weren't true. Ray liked saying, "Donny'll be okay. He's been in situations like this before."

Ma was a wreck. A counsellor was made available. When the counsellor lady called, Ma never called her back. Ma's work gave her time off and said they'd keep paying her. Said to take as much time as she wanted. After a week, Ma went back. Work, she told me, was the only thing she could do that made her think to about something other than Donny.

I was still studying at night in the dining room. I didn't want to disturb Ma, so for a couple weekends, Ray came over and we set up a place for me to study in the basement beside the furnace. When Ma wasn't around, we talked about Donny. We went to *Re-Use* and loaded the back of Ray's pickup with used material like wall panelling and two-by-fours. Where the desk was going to go, we laid a piece of worn brown carpet. Ray drilled into the cinder blocks to put up bookshelves. The washing machine had to be moved. Two-by-fours were anchored into the floor. A small room was framed in, but we never got around to putting the panelling up. Ray joked that it looked like a cage.

The basement was moldy. Ray said he'd keep his eyes peeled for a dehumidifier. I bought a desk from Goodwill and an electric typewriter. After I moved all my books and stuff downstairs, I realized it was too dark for reading. When I showed Ray, he wired in a light bulb to the joist above the desk

After a few months, the news about Donny was never different. Every so often, new photographs would be released. Around Halloween, I heard my humanities professor talking about Donny's situation with some students. I pretended I wasn't listening. About that time, the *Star* printed new photos. None of them looked like Donny anymore. A student with purple streaks in her hair pointed at the photos "Serves him right," she told the others. "Shouldn't be there anyways." A button pinned on the collar of her coat said *Imagine*.

They talked more about Donny until the prof closed the classroom door and everyone quieted down. Late students hurried in and took their seats. Chairs were dragged and boots scuffed the floor. Over the noise, someone behind me said to the girl with the purple streaks, "That guy's a goner."

Then at Christmastime, a video tape came out. I was in line at the Cock and Bull pub getting a coffee for lunch. The TV in the corner of the pub was on. The picture wasn't clear but I knew it was Donny. His eyes were swollen into slits. Kneeling, his arms were bound behind his back. Out of nowhere, he gets bashed in the head with the butt of a rifle. As he's falling sideways, he gets kicked in face by someone you can't really see. Stuff like black jelly sprays out of his mouth. There was no the sound. The volume was turned down. Before I could pay for the coffee, Donny getting his head bashed was shown three more times.

When all this was going on, Ray talked about moving back home. He really didn't want to, though. He figured he and his girlfriend Kim were going to get back together. Every few weeks, they'd split up. Ray talked to Ma about Kim all the time. He talked about her so they wouldn't have to talk about Donny.

When Kim told Ray she was having a kid, they moved in together. They got a place above The Today restaurant on the Danforth. You could get Greek or Ethiopian food there. The apartment stank like spices and cooking oil and meat. After Ray lived there for a while, he stank like that, too. Once, Ma ran into Kim on the subway. She told Ma Ray got her pregnant. That's how Ma found out. She promised Ma that if the baby was a boy, she'd name him *Donny* after Donny. If it was a girl, she'd name her *Tammy* because it almost sounded the same.

Kim was a head case. She was lying about the whole thing. There was no kid, but she went on about being pregnant for way longer than nine months. It didn't matter to her, though. She'd rub her stomach and talk to her belly and tell everyone how big this baby was going to be. She was just getting fat. When Ray found out the truth, she went to the cops and told them he was raping her. When they checked it out, she admitted she made it all up because she was dying from a few kinds of cancer and was afraid Ray was going to leave her. She came to the house one night looking for Ray. Pounding on the door, she was loud, screaming that Ray was a prick, that he made her get an abortion. I turned off the lights and pretended no one was home.

Donny got free at the end of February. Before he was brought back to Canada, he was taken to a hospital in Germany. Ma could've gone to see him. They would have flown her there. She had never been on an airplane before. She was too afraid. Ma was there a few days later when his plane landed at the base in Trenton.

An officer drove her. It was early in the morning when a car came to pick her up. It was a Crown-Victoria, grey with tinted windows. In the middle of the roof there was a short antenna, thin as a coat hanger. Ma got in the back. The officer got in beside her. Ray went around to the other side to get in but the door was locked.

The driver's window rolled slowly down. "Private Hogan has requested only his mother attend."

Ray squinted. He shook his head. "What the fuck does that mean?"

I tried the door handle on my side but it was locked, too. I couldn't see Ma through the tinted glass, only my reflection. I imagined her sitting rigid, straight, the smooth leather seat cold against her legs. Putting my face closer to the window, I imagined her small hands folded, resting motionless on her lap as she stared at the headrest in front of her.

She had to have known Donny didn't want Ray and me there, or she wouldn't have got in the car. She must have known but did not know how to tell us. As the car started to move, I stepped back. She wouldn't talk the whole way there. I knew she wouldn't.

As the Crown-Vic pulled away, its tires crushed the ice and grey snow banking the curb. Ray was standing in the middle of the road. In his hand, he held a gift he was going to take to Donny. When the car turned the corner, Ray tore off the wrapping paper and threw it away. He had wrapped two packs of cigarettes and a bottle of aftershave in Christmas paper.

"Here." He tossed a pack to me. He put the other one in his coat pocket.

Holding the cigarette pack back out toward Ray, I said, "Just wait and give 'em to him later."

Ray started up the driveway. I wasn't sure if he dropped it deliberately, or if it slipped, but the bottle of aftershave hit the pavement and shattered. "Who gives a shit," he said without stopping to pick up the shards. A wave of Brute-33 blew in my face.

Donny came back to Toronto but he couldn't come home. He was put in the Sunnybrook hospital, in the K-wing. They had a psyche ward for messed-up soldiers. Some had been in there since the Korean War.

The first time we went to visit him, we had to have a meeting with a social worker named Jody. She was about thirty, had long hair and nice eyes. She explained what happened to Donny when he was held captive. She explained his condition. "He's having a difficult time adjusting." She told us Donny only wanted Ma to go up to the room, but didn't explain why. The whole time she was talking, Ray was checking her out. When the meeting was over, Ma and I got up and thanked Jody and then left. Ray hung back a few minutes, saying he wanted to ask Jody one more thing.

Later, when Ma wasn't around, I asked him, "What'd you talk to that social worker lady about?"

Ray waved his hand, he scoffed, "Nothing. Just, umm, just asked her if she wanted to go out some time, like for a coffee or something."

"Really? What she say?"

"Said that wouldn't be *ethical* or some shit like that. Fucking lesbian."

Even though Ma was the only one who visited Donny, Ray and I still drove her to the hospital. While Ma was up in the room, we'd wait out in the parking lot, or sit around in the lobby. Sometimes I brought a book I had to read for class.

The patients were old. Black and Philipino nurses pushed them around in wheelchairs. The ones using walkers moved real slowly. Ray and I made bets on how long it would take them to cross the lobby.

Every time we went, we'd see this skinny old guy wandering around. His head looked like a dried-up apple. In some places his skull was caved in, like pieces of bone had been removed. No one had combed his thin hair in months. He had on nothing else but a blue smock. Tattoos on his wrinkled forearms had become blotches of faded navy blue ink. He'd come shuffling off the elevator in a pair of soiled slippers, look around the lobby, and if he spotted us, he'd come over to where we were sitting and talk to us as if we were people he knew.

When we'd see him coming Ray would say, "Here comes old *Crown-and-Anchor*." Sometimes we called him *Popeye*. Eventually, the same fat black nurse in a red uniform would come looking for him. With his shrivelled ass hanging out, she'd lead him back to the elevators, scolding him for leaving his floor.

Ray nudged me in the ribs, "Eh Mike, what war was that guy in?"

After a while, we stopped going to Sunnybrook. Ma took the bus there by herself.

A few days after my exams were done, I talked with Ray about Ma's idea of us working together. He said Ma had already mentioned it to him and he thought we could give it a go. Only one other time had the three of us ever worked together. That was the summer we had jobs at the Exhibition. All of our shifts were almost the same. At the end of the night, we'd meet at the back of the Food Building. Donny got his hands on a ring of keys that fit most of the locks. We'd go inside and rip stuff off. That was the best part of the job. Goofing around on the Bathurst 511 streetcar home, we'd pig out on pretzels and Pogos and deep-fried doughnuts.

Ray said he knew a guy who knew a contractor up in Markham who was always looking for workers. "Maybe he can help us out."

A few days later, Ray got through to the contractor. He had something for us, but he said he wanted to meet the guys who would be working on his jobs. He said he'd been screwed around too many times. That's what Ray told me.

Ray and I drove to the site. Construction was complete. It wasn't a big site, around thirty houses, but it appeared abandoned. There were no construction vehicles or workies anywhere, only huge brick houses surrounded by fields of muck, tired-rutted by heavy equipment. Roads were paved and the sidewalks poured, but that was it. Everything else was muddy. No lawns or shrubs anywhere. Like wooden matchsticks, stakes had been driven into the earth, their tips painted orange and red. Ray said eventually, that's where the trees would go. Trees were all over the place, but none of them had been put in the ground. The landscaper had dumped them at the front of the houses and along the curb and left them there. The branches were bare. Some had had their bark torn off. The roots and earth at their base were wrapped in tight skins of burlap. At the end of the street, a Johnny-On-The-Spot had been pushed over. Burnt skids piled two and three high littered the area around it.

At the rear of the site, in the middle of a muddy field was a white trailer, its windows papered over. It sat unevenly on blocks of concrete, one end sinking into the earth. Before we got out of the pickup, Ray said to let him do all the talking. As Ray banged on the trailer door with the side of his fist, I stood behind him scraping muck off my boots.

There was no answer. Ray put his mouth close to the door, "Mr. Greenfield?" No reply. He banged harder. We waited. Putting his hand to his mouth, Ray leaned into the door and yelled "Mr. Greenfield? You in there? I spoke with you on the phone. It's Raymond Hogan about painting."

Something struck the inside of the trailer door. Startled, we both stepped backward. Greenfield hollered, "What are youse waiting for, a feckin' invitation? Get in here." There was about two pounds of mud stuck on our boots. We did our best to scrape it off quickly on the wooden step. It didn't help much.

The air inside the trailer was stuffy. It smelled like soiled clothing, stale cigarette smoke and shit. Greenfield was seated in a swivel chair behind a desk doing his fly up. The floor sloped on an angle toward one end of the trailer. The wheels on his chair had been removed. It was like being in the funhouse at the Ex. At the bottom end of the trailer, in the corner, there was a cot and beside that, a five-gallon paint can. Piled close by on a stool were a stack of magazines. Sitting on top of them were rolls of toilet paper.

Ray introduced himself. Then he introduced me. We sat in plastic chairs opposite Greenfield. The seats, their backs, even the chrome legs were caked in mud. The top of Greenfield's desk was barely visible for all the garbage piled on it. Food wrappers. Binders and clipboards. Coffee cups. An overflowing ashtray. The white brim of a crushed plastic workie helmet peeked out from beneath a heap of yellowed papers.

By the way Greenfield spoke, it was hard to tell if he had an accent or just a speech impediment. From working outdoors, his skin was permanently tanned. His eyes were huge, green and bloodshot. He had no hair. There was a scar down the middle of his scalp, like a long time ago someone had brought a hatchet down hard into his skull. His head looked like the shell of a hard-boiled brown egg that split from being boiled too long, the grey ooze hardened into scar tissue.

Greenfield rubbed his forehead when he spoke. "Feckin' sod bastards. Two weeks late. Homeowners are all up my arse-hole. Then the municipality goes and issued a stop-work order 'cause of a little small sinkhole— What the feck do youse two want?"

Ray reminded him about their phone conversation. "Oh. Right. Youse two aren't *eye-ties*, are you? Don't sub to *wops*. Had enough with them."

Ray didn't answer. I wasn't going to. Greenfield finished, "Youse don't look *Eye*-talian."

Greenfield got around to telling us he had some suites downtown, two, maybe three that the property management he did work for wanted painted. "Can either of youse paint?" he asked.

Ray spoke up. "Sure, anyone can paint." I shrugged. I didn't like Greenfield. I wanted to leave.

"Yeah, sure, *anyone* can paint," Greenfield snapped. He put his hands behind his head and leaned back in the chair. Veins bulged and pulsed like snakes writhing beneath the tight skin of his temples. "*Anyone's* fecked up a lot of jobs for me too, and *any-one's* cost me a lot of feckin' dough."

I didn't like the way Greenfield went off. If it weren't for Ray, I would have got up and left. Looking down at the drying muck on my boots, I scalped the sole against the chair legs. I thought of Ma and Donny and figured I'd just sit tight. I was glad Ray had said he'd do all the talking. Nothing happened for a few minutes. We sat and stared at Greenfield until he calmed down and went back to rubbing his forehead. Outside, the wind rattled the sides of the trailer. "'Kay," he said eventually, "I'll give youse a go."

There were some suites in a hotel that was being renovated he wanted us to paint. The hotel was downtown, near the bus station. It used to be a Holiday Inn until some Arabs bought it and renamed it, The Jordon. The Jordon rented suites to businessmen staying in Toronto for a month or two. Every suite had a kitchenette. They could make their own food.

"Thing is, they're lookin' for good work. Nothing sloppy. No hacks."

While Greenfield and Ray talked about the paint, what sort of finish they wanted, when we'd start, how we'd get paid, I went into my jacket for a smoke. Out of the blue, Greenfield went off again. "What the feck is wrong with your brother?" He slammed both fists on the desk sending up a cloud of dust, butts jumping over the rim of the ashtray. "Was he dragged up in a barn? Can't you feckin' read?" He jerked his thumb backward over his shoulder. We looked to see what he was pointing at. There was a nail stuck in the wall. Ray and I looked at each other and then around the trailer. Greenfield kept jabbing his thumb over his shoulder. There was no No Smoking sign any where on the wall behind him. It was lying on the trailer floor, near the door. Sliding the cigarette back into the pack, I slouched in my chair, biting the inside of my mouth.

The deal Greenfield gave us was good. We'd make enough cash to split three ways. With Ray's pickup, we wouldn't have to worry about getting around. The only part I didn't like was Greenfield's final condition. He said he had a nephew that would be working with us.

I drove us back home. Ray sat beside me smoking and making plans. He figured there were more suites that needed painting, but first Greenfield wanted to see our work. I was thinking about the nephew.

"Don't worry about the nephew," Ray explained, "guys like him never show."

When we got to the house, we told Ma about The Jordon. She was happy. She said a social worker lady came by to talk to her and see where Donny would be living.

"Was it that one, Jody?" Ray interrupted.

Ma said, "No, it was a different one."

Ma told us Donny would be allowed to come home soon. She started crying a bit. Ray and me didn't know what to do. Ray tore a few pieces of paper towel off the roll and handed them to her so she'd stop. Donny needed his own room. Even though my room had two beds, Ma asked me if I could sleep on the chesterfield for a while or maybe stay at Ray's.

"Mikey can stay with me. Kim won't care—"

I cut him off, "No, don't worry, I'll sleep in the living room. Donny can have the bed for as long as he wants it."

"Why doesn't Donny stay with me? When Kim comes back, I'll tell her to find another place to stay for a while."

Ma said no, everything's been set up with the social worker.

A week or so later, Donny was still in Sunnybrook. Ray and I got started at The Jordon. There was no sign of Greenfield's nephew. The suites were small. Ray and me bumped into each other. I was clumsy. I stepped in a full tray of paint. Ray showed me how to cut and how to roll.

The first suite took longer to paint than Ray figured. "We lost on this one. But don't worry, we'll go through the next one quicker." He was right. We got into a routine. We were staying out of each other's way. When I'd be rolling the kitchenette, Ray would cut the closet. Painting was better than working at Coke. We were making good money and they kept giving us more suites. One afternoon, Greenfield came by. Ray and I were folding drop sheets, the walls and door frames still wet with beige paint.

"Feckin' Arabs. They like your work. They want every suite done." Greenfield dragged his thumb along the wall. He wiped wet paint on his pants. "Youse struck gold." He went to the window, the glass framed floor to ceiling. Looking down at the street, he opened a pair of chrome nail clippers and using the file, picked at the dirt jammed under his fingernails. Laughing, he turned to us, his lips curled back above his teeth, "Guess youse are going to be paintin' for the rest of your feckin' lives." When he laughed, I noticed his gums had turned black.

The Jordon was nineteen stories. There were three hundred and five suites. By then, we'd painted six. At break, Ray and I would sit by the huge window and have a smoke and a coffee. Some of the suites were non-smoking. The Jordon has no balconies. When we did those ones, we'd go in the stairwell and smoke. None of the windows opened.

At lunch, we move five-gallon pails of paint closer to the window and eat sandwiches we brought from home. With our elbows resting on our knees, we'd sit, foreheads pressed against the soundproof glass and look out over the city. A bloated skin of yellow haze blanketed the sky like a layer of fat. Roofs were a mess of antennas and sun-bleached satellite dishes discoloured by pigeon shit. Except for the buildings that were taller than The Jordon, from up here, we could see over everything. We could see over streets, alleys, delivery trucks and Greyhound buses discharging black mushrooms of exhaust. Fire trucks blocking traffic, construction crews, police cruisers parked partially on sidewalks, taxis all over the place, and men and women dressed up for work who always seemed in a hurry no matter what time it was. In the distance, Toronto ended abruptly at the lake.

We could see everything, but there wasn't any sound. Like in memory, the city moved in silence.

Other times, we'd just play cards.

"Ya have any fives?"

"Fish. Ma said Donny's coming home tomorrow, for sure. She told me last night. Ya got any kings?"

Ray put his cards down on his knee and poured black coffee from a dented thermos into the plastic lid.

I told him, "Fish."

He asked if I wanted some coffee. I shook my head. Instead of taking my turn, I waited for him to finish telling me what else Ma said.

He picked up his cards and studied them. "Ma said Donny'll be coming to work with us on Monday or Tuesday. The sooner things get back to normal Ma said, the better." Ray took a sip of coffee. "That's what Ma said. Ya got any sevens?"

Ray and I hadn't seen Donny or spoken to him in a long time. When Donny had finished his courses in electrical at George Brown, he needed to apprentice somewhere, but could not find work. I'm not sure how, but he hooked up with some guys at the Moss Park Armoury. The recruitment officer there told him that experience in a signals corps would be considered apprenticing. It took a while for Donny to convince Ma. The recruitment officer told him to tell her all that bullshit about Canadians being peacekeepers. Besides, 6th Field Engineer Regiment had been designated *un-deployable*. The furthest he'd probably be sent was Edmonton or Gagetown. Ma didn't like the idea much, but she came around. The day Donny signed up, Ma was there. It was okay for a while until things went got hot in the Middle East. The 6th were one of the first regiments deployed.

We got back to work and didn't stop. It was Friday so we finished early and left The Jordon before three. We could do that

because we were working for ourselves. I liked that. Ray took out
a roll of twenties and gave me my part in cash. When I got home,
I put half in an envelope for Ma.

Donny came home Sunday. He came in a taxi by himself. I was in
the basement, reading. In the morning before he came home, Ma
was nervous. She got up early and put clean sheets on my bed for
Donny. For the rest of the morning, she sat at the kitchen table
drinking tea. I couldn't be around her but I didn't want to leave
her alone.

Halfway down the basement stairs, I called out, "I'll be downstairs."

Setting the tea cup on the table, I could barely hear her when
she asked softly, "How do we act around him, Mike? When we're
together, what do we say?"

I stopped on the bottom step. "Nothing Ma, just do what we
normally do."

"Act like everything's normal?"

"Yeah. I guess."

Later, on the floor above me, I heard Donny drop his bag and
Ma walking around the dining room and the kitchen. Ma made
tea. I could only hear her talking. Later in the afternoon, I heard
Ray's voice but I still didn't go up. A couple of times, the screen
door out to the backyard squeaked opened and closed. The house
went quiet. When I went up, Donny and Ray were out back sitting at the picnic bench. I hesitated behind the screen door, my
hand on the latch. Ma had come in to get something. She nudged
me from behind. "Go out there Mike. Go say *hi* to him."

Donny's back was to me and the sun was in Ray's eyes.
Donny's hair was cut too short, exposing the pink flesh of his

scalp. From beneath his long-sleeved shirt, shoulder blades rose into sharp points. Ma was standing beside me. She saw I was staring at the bones that showed in Donny's head. Tendons stretched like rigid bands of rubber down the back of his neck.

Shit, he's thin.

Ma started crying, her voice unsteady. "Look at him. What did they do to him?"

Biting the inside of my mouth, I realized looking at Donny and Ray, nothing could be normal again. For three hundred and five days, Donny was chained up. He was beaten. His head was dunked under water until he couldn't breathe. They raped him with a flashlight.

When I went outside, Ray was telling Donny about The Jordon. He was talking slow like Donny didn't understand English. Donny sat motionless, listening, his back perfectly straight, shoulders squared.

The sun was hot. I felt heat upon my face. Beads of perspiration glinting on his forehead, Ray was in cutoff denim shorts and a T-shirt. The buttons on Donny's long-sleeve shirt were done up, including the cuffs and the collar. Moving slow like his body was submerged in water, he reached for the cold glass of lemonade Ma kept refilling, and sipped. When I came beside him, he turned and stared up at me. Holding the glass pressed to his lips, condensation soaked his fingers. His eyes were dull, clouded by the medication he'd been prescribed. Beneath this, I glimpsed a flash of anguish.

Ray stopped talking. Donny set the glass down on the picnic table. Extending his hand toward me like he intended to shake mine, he changed his mind and pulled it back. Swinging his legs over the bench, he got up from the picnic table. I avoided his eyes. Like it was normal to, I put my arms around him. I could feel his ribs, his spine, his collar bone. We didn't saying anything. I looked at the rings of condensation where Donny's glass has scarred the picnic table, watching them evaporate before my eyes and trying not to think about the things that had happened to him.

On Monday we took Donny to The Jordon. We showed him around. With three of us painting, it took time to get into a new routine. For a while we bumped into one another or had to wait for a ladder or to move a drop sheet. Small things like that. At lunch and at break the three of us would sit on five-gallon pails of paint and smoke, talk and have coffees or just look out the window.

We played crazy eights or fish.

Greenfield came by asking if we'd seen his nephew. We had not. Greenfield's nephew's name was Malcolm. He was Greenfield's sister's son, and he owed her a favour. Before he explained any more, Greenfield asked who Donny was.

"Donny, come out here for one sec." Donny was in the closet, cutting. Greenfield waved his hand over his head. He was in a hurry, he said he didn't have time. Turning, his hand was on the door handle when Donny appeared. Donny had been working with us for a couple of weeks. He was nearly back to his normal weight. None of his bones were poking out from under his shirt. He still wouldn't roll up his sleeves or wear shorts, though.

I said to Greenfield, "This is my other brother, Donny."

"Wow." Greenfield sized Donny up. "Aren't you the big feckin' boy," Greenfield said, extending his hand. Donny clenched a paintbrush at his side. His other hand remained closed. He said, "Hmm." He nodded and went back to the closet.

Greenfield shook his head. Opening the door, he stepped into the hall and started to say something about his nephew, but the door swung closed before he could finish.

After work, Ray would drop Donny and I at home. If Ma was there, she'd be at the window or on the porch, waiting. Ma and Ray kept telling me Donny was getting better. Besides gaining weight, they said, his hair was growing back. For a while, he had been losing it in patches. Ma thought it was just his sleep that wasn't so good. If he could only get a good night sleep, she'd tell me, her voice lowered to a whisper, he'd feel much better. He woke Ma and me up, banging around in my old bedroom, shouting and sobbing in his sleep.

I wasn't allowed in my bedroom anymore, except to get clean clothes. The rest of the time the door stayed closed. At night, he'd wedge a chair under the doorknob so none of us could get in. When he and Ma were out in the backyard, or when he was in the bathroom, I'd sneak in and get clean clothes. The way blankets and sheets were piled on the floor, I could tell that Donny slept in the closet.

Ma didn't think it was a big deal. "Ma, it's not normal. You should tell his worker."

Ma said no. "They might take him back to Sunnybrook," she whispered.

Some nights, Donny would crawl around the house in the dark in his underwear. Startled awake, the metallic taste of sleep coating my tongue, Donny would be crunched somewhere in the darkened living room. I'd hear him panting hard and short breaths. In the minute it took for my eyes to adjust to the black, I'd watch him scurry through the razors of light which pierced the window from the streetlamp outside. Flashes of perspiration glistened on his pale forehead. Lying perfectly still, I didn't swallow or move at all. When I could finally make things out, I'd follow him with my eyes as he crept low to the floor. I was never sure if he was awake or asleep. One time, he came up beside the chesterfield. His face close to mine, breathing slowed, controlled, he laid his hand across my throat. I wanted to fill the darkness with my voice but I was too afraid. I wanted to say his name, but I didn't think it was Donny anymore. Before he did anything else, he lowered himself and crept away. Eyes wide open, he looked back, again and again like he was being chased, like he was crawling out of a nightmare.

After this happened a few times, I started sleeping in the basement beside my desk. On a Saturday afternoon when Donny and Ray were playing cards in the backyard, I dragged the mattress off the other bed and took it downstairs.

Suite No. 1818 was done. It was Friday. Management let us store our equipment in the suites. On Mondays, they'd give Ray a list of the next dozen suites to be painted. The order they went in didn't make sense. Even if two suites on the same floor were to be done, we wouldn't paint them one after the other. Instead, we'd start in No. 802, paint it, move all our shit up to the to the fourteenth floor, paint No. 1411, go down to the second floor, paint a suite there, and then go back up to the eighth floor where we'd been three days earlier. I told Ray it was a stupid way of doing things. Why not finish all the suites that were on the same floor, then move to the next one?

"That's the way they want them done," Ray said, waving the list, "so that's the way we'll do 'em." Seemed to me, working it the way they wanted, we always ended up back where we started, just one suite over.

Donny and I were folding drop sheets. Ray was in the bathroom cleaning brushes in the tub. Turning the water off, he shook the brushes to get the water out. As he did, he asked us if we wanted to stop somewhere for a drink before going home. I said I'd go,

if Donny was going. Donny said no. Besides coming to The
Jordon, Donny never went anywhere, except out in the backyard
at home.

"Come on, Don, just a beer, or you don't even have to have a
beer. Have a pop or ginger ale or something." Ray called him *Don*.
Ray hardly ever called Donny that. By the way he was going on, I
could tell Ma had put Ray up to asking. Ray wouldn't let it go.
"Come on, Don, what do ya say? A ginger ale? At that place on
Donlands, you know, the place that shows Leafs games."

"No. I wanna go home."

We washed up. Ray and me went into the bathroom together.
Beside each other, leaning over the small sink, our elbows bumped
as we splash water on our faces, scrubbed paint off our hands and
arms. The tile floor got soaked. We put on clean white T-shirts.
When it was Donny's turn, he went in and locked the door. He
took his time, putting the plug in the drain, filling the sink with
hot water. He washed his face, hands, picked flecks of stucco out
of his hair. When he came out, his face was blotchy from the hot
water. His hair was combed to the side. Even though Ma gave him
a clean shirt, he was still wearing the long-sleeved work shirt he
painted in. The front was smeared with beige paint, white caulk-
ing.

The Jordon gave us a parking spot in their underground
garage. It was humid outside, but down there, the air was cool and
smelled like exhaust. Near the pickup, Ray tossed me the keys.
"You drive," he said. Turning the ignition, the engine started but
the gas gauge didn't move. It stayed on empty. I told Ray we
needed gas. Ray sat between us, a lit cigarette burning in the corner of his mouth. He was trying to get something on the radio.
"Nah, don't worry," he said without looking away from the dial,
"It's the gauge. It's always on empty."

Traffic was slow. There was construction. It was stop-and-go until we got across the Bloor Street viaduct. It was hot inside the pickup. The handle on the driver's side window didn't turn properly. The glass rolled down only halfway. I asked Donny to open his window, but he ignored me.

The whole time we were driving, Ray kept trying to convince Donny to say yes about stopping for a drink. While waiting for a green at Chester, Ray said, "Let's go to The Gonny." That was a bar on Donlands. Its real name was The Gondola. People like Ray who drank there called it The Gonny. Everyone else called it The Gonor, short for gonorrhea. That's where Ray met Kim.

The light turned green. "Just for a little while, Donny. What do ya say? It's early. There's no ballgame on. There won't hardly be anyone there. It's not far." Ray turned to me, "Mikey, make a left at Donlands."

"But Donny said he don't want to," I replied. "Let's just go home."

Gripping the armrest on the door panel, Donny stared out the front windshield and said, "Yeah, I wanna go home."

A small, orange light on the dash below the gas gauge flashed. "Hey Ray, what's that mean?"

"I don't know. It's never done that before."

There was an Esso station up ahead on the other side of the road. I put on the indicator to make a left. Suddenly starved of fuel, the pickup began to jerk, the engine sputtered. I figured we had enough speed and were close enough that we'd be able to coast up to the pumps. The light up ahead was red. No traffic was coming toward us. I shifted into neutral, killed the engine and we began to roll. When I checked the mirrors, I saw Donny's eyes darting all over the place. He looked confused. Rubbing his hands on his kneecaps, he swallowed continuously, his Adam's apple rising and sinking like something stuck in his throat.

When I started making the turn, Donny reached across and yanked the steering wheel toward him. It happened so fast, I tried to steer straight, but couldn't. The pickup weaved all over the road. Ray grabbed Donny's wrist and tried pulling it away. The pickup veered toward the curb. In the back of the truck, paint cans and buckets, busted extension poles and a ladder slid back and forth, ricocheting off the sides of the box.

With his hand clutching Donny's arm, Ray yelled, "What the fuck are you doin' Donny? Let it go, let Mikey drive."

Donny's grip tightened. A tangle of veins pulsed blue and purple on the back of his hand. I pressed hard on the brakes. The truck stopped abruptly. The three of us went forward and then back, hard against the bench seat. A horn blared. A taxi swerved around us. The front of the pickup came close to knocking a lady off her bicycle. All around us, tires screeched. We were blocking two lanes. People on the sidewalk stared. Customers seated at outdoor cafés turned. Drivers laid on their horns and wouldn't let up. Over all the noise, a delivery guy leaned out his truck window, "What are you, a fuckin' idiot? Learn to drive."

Like he was watching something happening far away, Donny froze, his sight fixed on a thing only he could see. Ray pulled at his arm. It wouldn't budge. Ray tried prying his fingers off the steering wheel. Ray got pissed and hauled on Donny's wrist. Buttons on the cuff of Donny's shirt popped off, the sleeve tearing back to his elbow.

The noise around us seemed to disappear. Donny's arm was a mess. Fingernail-size scars pocked his skin where cigarettes had been put out. From being bound for such a long time, his wrist was permanently bruised light purple, the flesh worn nearly to the bone. Zigzagging scars outlined where tattoos on his forearm had been carved out.

Donny let the steering wheel go. Pulling the sleeve down over his wrist, he placed one hand in the other and rested them on his lap. None of us spoke. Wiping his brow, he took a deep breath, exhaled and said, "Take me home."

Around the middle of August, it got humid. Even at night it stayed sticky. It wasn't so bad for sleeping because the basement was cool. The Jordon was air-conditioned and things were going good. We were knocking off two and three suites in a day and the money was great. After a while though, it got boring. The suites were identical. They were painted two different colours, beige and a colour a bit lighter than beige, called honey beige.

Every so often, Greenfield would come by. Sometimes he brought coffees. Looking around at our work, he nodded and said we were pretty good. If we ever finished at The Jordon, he had other jobs to give us. Before he left, he asked if Malcolm had been by.

Ray shook his head, "Nope. No sign of him."

When Greenfield was gone, we'd talk about Malcolm like he was someone we knew, someone none of us liked. Donny said it would be real shitty if he ever showed up.

Ray insisted, "Guy's an asshole, I'll guarantee it; he ain't coming."

I pictured Malcolm like his uncle, only younger, but with the same bashed-in head, bad teeth and black gums. "You think this Malcolm guy looks like Greenfield?" Donny and Ray looked at me kind of funny. "I mean, if he's ugly, ya know, like his uncle."

Donny chuckled, "What are you, a fuckin' fag, Mikey? Who cares what he looks like, long as he never shows up. Why should we have to split money with that asshole?"

"I'm telling ya, he's never going to show," Ray promised.

"Yeah, you're probably right," I agreed.

Ray and Kim made up and Donny was getting better. He still wouldn't wear anything that wasn't long-sleeved and he always wore pants, but on Saturdays, he and Ma would go shopping for groceries. They'd walk all the way over to the Mister Grocer's on Strathmore. Pushing the shopping cart a few steps behind her, Donny followed her up and down the aisles while Ma bought the stuff we needed.

For Ma's birthday, we went to Swiss Chalet. To make up for bringing Kim, Ray said the meal was on him. Most of the dinner, Kim was in a bad mood. She hardly talked. She stuffed her face with French fries and chewed ice from her Coke. When her food was done, she ate off Ray's plate and gave our waitress dirty looks each time she passed the table. Ray waited until Kim went to the bathroom and then he told us his idea about us registering as a real company. We'd get business cards with our names printed on them.

"We start with the painting, but eventually we get bigger," Ray said, reminding us that Greenfield had mentioned more work.

As Ray was speaking, Ma sat beside him, nodding and listening. She smiled. She liked that idea, she said. I could tell by the way she was acting that the two of them had talked about it already. Donny scoffed down a mouthful of chicken. Wiping grease off his chin with the back of his hand, he said that he liked Ray's idea, too.

Ma poured sauce on her sandwich. Without looking up, she asked, "What about you, Mike?"

The three of them stopped eating. I reminded them about school. I was already registered for my courses. "I go back in three weeks, but I'll still do the painting part-time, if you want."

Picking up her serviette, Ma dabbed her mouth and then absentmindedly folded the serviette in half. She folded it a second time and placed it beside her plate. Without looking at me, all she said was, "Oh."

Back at home, Ma opened her gifts. The *After Eights* I bought her were melted. Ray got her a purse. Donny didn't give her anything.

The day we started No. 305, Malcolm showed up. In the morning when we got there, he was sitting on a five-gallon pail of paint, looking out the window. At first, we figured it was one of The Jordon's maintenance guys hiding from management in the empty suite. They did that sometimes.

When he heard the door, he stood, and as he came toward us, he said, "My uncle said to come here. He said I'd be workin' with youse." He pointed his finger at us, "Who's Ray?"

Ray sighed, "I am."

Malcolm looked about the same age as Ray, only he was black. He was wearing clean overalls, a white T-shirt, and a painter's cap. Bristles of coarse, dark hair grew from his chin.

"Hey." He shook Ray's hand, "I'm Malcolm."

Donny cracked, "Yeah. We know."

Standing in the small entrance, we stared at each other. None of us said anything until Donny chuckled.

"What's funny?" Malcolm moved in close to Donny.

Donny told him, "Nothing. Just didn't expect you to be a—"

Ray piped in, "—for you be here, this morning. And well, you know, Greenfield's, umm. Your uncle's a white guy, and umm. We weren't expecting you to be, you know, *black*." Ray added quickly, "It's okay, though."

"I know it's okay." Tilting his head back as though he was smelling something, Malcolm added, "'Cause my uncle's the boss." When he smiled, I noticed how white his teeth were.

We got to work and skipped the morning break. At lunch, Malcolm went down to buy something to eat. Donny and Ray and I ate lunch and said next to nothing. Instead of playing cards, we finished and got right back to painting.

The suite was too small for the four of us. It took longer to get done because we were in each other's way. At the end of the day, Malcolm asked Ray if we'd drop him at the subway. Before Ray could answer, Donny told him there wasn't enough room in the truck.

By week's end, Ray had decided it would be better if we split up into pairs. While we were taking turns washing up, he told us that starting Monday, Malcolm and I would be working together in one suite while him and Donny painted another.

Ray knew I was sort of pissed. "Don't worry, we'll still have breaks and lunch together," he said.

Over the weekend, he went to the paint store and bought more equipment. Monday morning he divided the list of suites in two, writing down the ones Malcolm and I would be doing.

When he wasn't talking, Malcolm was actually a pretty good painter. Since high school, he had been working as a general labourer for his uncle. After we'd set up our equipment and put down the drop sheets, he'd spend a lot of time walking around with a clean paintbrush in his hand, talking and looking out the window while I cut or rolled. Mostly, he talked about the track and betting on horses. I found out Greenfield once had a horse stabled at Woodbine until he was charged with something called *cheating at playing.* It was a few years back. Greenfield was having money trouble. An opportunity to fix things in his horse's favour presented itself. Malcolm was involved. In the end, Greenfield lost track privileges and was banned from Woodbine for life. Because Malcolm had other priors, he did twenty-one months at the East Detention Centre.

Malcolm had this thing about betting. At first, I didn't pay much attention to it, but after a while, it started bugging me. Most of his sentences began, *Betcha this* or *I'll betcha that.* It was too much. While we'd be painting, the radio would be on and he'd yell from the bedroom or the kitchenette, "Mike, betcha I can tell the next song they'll play." What did I care? I wouldn't respond. At lunch, he'd bet he could guess what kind of meat we'd put in our sandwiches.

"Come on, boys, betcha a dollar, okay, a quarter, what do ya say?" We just shook our heads and started eating our lunch.

"Okay, fine. A gentleman's bet."

Unwrapping his sandwich, Donny told Malcolm to shut up and eat.

Ray got out the cards. "What should I deal, fish or crazy eights?"

"How 'bout three-card monte."

"How 'bout, dominos? Betcha like to play dominos, eh Malcolm?" Donny sipped his coffee. "Black guys all like playing dominos, right?"

Ray put the cards away. "Forget it. Let's get back to work."

Driving home, Ray told Donny to stop making cracks about Malcolm being black.

"I don't really care what colour he is, Ray," Donny stated, "I just wish he'd leave."

The two of them went back and forth like this. Ray was driving. I sat between them and kept my mouth shut.

"Think about it, Donny. Greenfield won't give us anymore work if his nephew goes back and tells him how we're going on about him being black." Donny stared out the window.

At the house, after I got out of the truck, I turned back to Ray and told him he could take a turn painting with Malcolm. Donny was standing on the curb. Ma was sitting on the porch. It was too hot in the house to stay inside. Ma waved.

Shifting into park, Ray told me to just sit tight, then leaning forward so Donny could hear him too, he said, "Malcolm's the kind of guy who'll show up for a couple days more then fall off the face of the earth. Just wait. We won't see him after a while."

"But it's been more than a week," I protested.

Donny squinted, the sun shining directly in his eyes. "Wait? I say we just get rid of 'im. Tell him we don't want 'im working with us no more."

"Didn't you hear what I said, Don?" Ray sighed, "If we wanna get work from Greenfield, we gotta put up with Malcolm for a while."

"What do ya mean, *we*? You guys just see him at break and at lunch. I spend the whole fuckin' day with him."

Ma started down the steps toward us. By the time she got to the sidewalk, I was already in the house.

Ray must have got Ma to talk to Donny about Malcolm, because over the next few days, I could see Donny was trying.

Shuffling a deck of cards, Ray asked what he should deal.

As he moved a pail of paint closer to us, Malcolm complained, "I played fish and crazy eights when I was kid. Why don't we play something else?"

Donny asked him, "Like what?"

"7's-take-all? Betcha boys are too scared of losin' your money to me."

"No," Donny said, "we're already losing money 'cause of you."

Ray threw a look at Donny.

Donny told us, "I know a game we can play. It's called basra." He said he learned it when he was in the Golan.

"The *Golan*? Where the fuck's that?" Malcolm laughed.

"Nowhere. Let me show *youse* how to play it." Donny replied.

For the rest of lunch, Donny tried showing us how to play basra. It was played in pairs. Naturally, I was paired with Malcolm. Donny was dealer. Player on the right of the dealer, that was always Ray, cut the deck, showed the card, dropped it face-up on the floor. Next, Donny dealt us four cards each. Cards were dropped, face-up.

We followed Donny's instructions, each dropping a card. Donny studied the cards on the parquet floor, "Okay," he explained, pointing at the four cards, "Ray's and mine's is higher, so we capture the basra. That's what ya call it when you win a round, *capturing the basra*." He reached down, collected the cards, slid them to the side toward Ray. "When you capture the basra, the cards go in your capture pile." For each capture, you got points. No matter what, seven of diamonds and jacks capture everything. First pair with a hundred points was the winner. There were a bunch of other rules. Donny had to explain them to us over and over.

At one point, as he was dealing out the cards, his cuff pulled back off his wrist. Malcolm caught it. "Whoa! Fuck man, what happened there?"

Donny straightened. He tugged at his cuffs. Clearing his throat, he said, "You know, Malcolm, I was like you once." He paused for a second, thinking about what he wanted to say. Nodding, he continued, "I was. No bullshit."

Malcolm shook his head. "What are you going on about?"

Donny leaned into Malcolm's face, but Malcolm didn't back off, the brim of his painter's cap nearly touching Donny's forehead. Ray's eyes darted between the two of them.

"Yeah, I was just like you, Malcolm, just, just hangin' around. But after a while, I realized, it was time for me to go. So when— When an *opportunity* presented itself, I took it and I left."

"What? What are you talking about? What's your point?"

"Malcolm, *bro'*, you ought to learn when it's time to go." Donny picked up the deck and finished dealing.

None of us could figure out Donny's game so we played a round of fish then got back to painting.

Later, in front of the house, after Donny and I got out of the pickup, Ray called me back. Donny was halfway up the driveway talking to Ma. Speaking over the idling engine, Ray told me maybe it would be better if Malcolm didn't have breaks and lunch with us.

I thought it was a good idea, too. Leaning in through the passenger-side window, I asked, "How we goin' manage that, though?"

Pretending to be watching something in the side-view mirror, Ray avoided looking at me. "What about if you and him just have your breaks and lunches together in the suite you two are painting in?"

I asked, "Are you for real?"

Ray wouldn't look at me. "Yeah."

After that, my time at The Jordon was spent alone with Malcolm. It really didn't matter anymore. I was sick of painting. Soon,

I'd be back at university. I already picked up my reading list. Ray told me I could work part-time at The Jordon and on all the other jobs Greenfield had. I never told Ray, but I had already spoken to my old supervisor at Coke. He said he'd do what could to get me on shifts.

"Have you talked to Greenfield?" I asked Ray. "What other work does he got?"

"He's got more jobs, but he wants Malcolm to keep working with us."

"What are you going to do?"

"Keep Greenfield happy but get rid of Malcolm. I wish we could tell him to just hit the road, but we can't. Donny and me got a few ideas about getting him to leave on his own."

Sometimes through the day, I'd have to go down to the suite Ray and Donny where in to get more paint or a brush, or something like that. Ray told me never to send Malcolm for anything. If I was hanging around too long talking or having a smoke, Ray would say "Hurry up, get back up there before Malcolm comes lookin' for you."

One morning while I was rolling a bathroom, Malcolm asked straight out, "What's wrong with your brother?" He leaned against the door frame, arms crossed, waiting for my answer. I kept painting.

"He was *in*, wasn't he? I can tell. He's got that *yardy* stare. There were guys like him in the East. Everyone called them *Yard Zombies*, or just *Yardies*. Just doin' their time, straight ahead, not wanting any trouble." Malcolm tried to whistle.

"Don't talk. Don't do nothin'. I remember Yardies like Donny. Actually, they'd rather spend all their time locked up. But the badges force 'em out to the yard for fifteen minutes at least so they can have their cells tossed. Yardies stay outta everything. Never talk hardly to no one, ever, all the time just starin' at something far away in their heads."

Malcolm played with the hairs on his chin. "I can just see Donny now, out in the yard in orange coveralls, leaning up against a wall, or just sittin' on the bench, alone. Guys like him do time up here." Malcolm tapped the side of his head. "Betcha that's it, ain't it? But what's the deal with his wrists?"

"No, Malcolm, that ain't it at all."

"Hey Mike, betcha maybe me and Donny could've been in the East at the same time, eh?"

I told him to get to work. Instead, he went over to the big window and stood in front of it for a while. I finished the bathroom and had started painting the kitchenette when all of a sudden Malcolm clapped his hands together once.

"Fuck me!" he called out, "I know who your brother is." Malcolm stood in the entrance to the kitchenette. "I remember him from the news. He was that guy those Pakis were holding, for like, a year or something."

Setting my brush into the paint pot, I leaned against the counter, staring at Malcolm. I didn't know what to say. I wished he hadn't remembered, but I really didn't care anymore. "They weren't Pakistani," I said, correcting him.

I'm not sure why, but I told Malcolm a little about what happen to Donny. Stuff the social worker told me.

"Donny was out stringing aerial wire with soldiers from the Italian corps of engineers and some peacekeepers from Bangladesh. The vehicle Donny was travelling in got separated from the others. They got lost, or got a flat or ran out of gas. Anyway, the Italians split on foot. Donny and one of the guys from Bangladesh were ambushed. They were captured. The people who had them never said why they were being held. There were no demands, not even a ransom. A couple of times Donny tried to get away, but he just ended up being caught and tortured more."

"Shit. What about the other guy?"

"What other guy?"

"The other soldier. The Paki from Bangladesh."

I had never thought of the other guy who was taken with Donny before. I'd imagined Donny alone the whole time. I shrugged, "Who knows?"

Picking up my brush, I cut a line of paint along the wall above the counter.

"How'd he get freed?"

I didn't feel like telling Malcolm anymore. I put more paint on the brush and continued cutting. "After a while, they just let him go," I lied.

That wasn't what really happened. One night, the people holding Donny were sitting around smoking and talking, probably playing basra and sipping rosewater. Somewhere in the same building, Donny was lying on his side on a dirty mattress, his hands tied behind his back. Some of the people left and the others must have fallen asleep because unlike every other night, no one came to check on Donny.

Working at the material around his wrists, Donny managed to get loose. He waited for hours before making a move. The only person guarding him was a fourteen-year-old girl wearing sandals. She had been left with an unloaded Kalashnikov and told to stay awake.

Outside the room Donny was kept in, the long hallway was lit by a single kerosene lamp. Donny waited until the girl guarding him dozed off. On his hands and knees, he crawled up behind her. He covered her mouth then choked her until she stopped moving. Donny bashed her skull in with the butt of the rifle.

The news never told that part. All they said was Donny was found by French peacekeepers on a pre-dawn patrol stumbling through the old part of the city in his underwear.

The rags Ray and me were using to clean the mess I'd made were sopping with paint. We were kneeling on the living-room floor. Malcolm and Donny were looking down at something out the window and talking.

Loud enough for only me to hear, Ray said out of the side of his mouth, "Why'd you let him come up?"

I whispered back, "What am I, his babysitter? I told him just to wait, that I'd be back down in a minute."

Malcolm and me had been finishing No. 604. We ran out of paint. Before I went to get another gallon, I told Malcolm to sit tight. When I left, he was at the window, looking out over the city.

Donny and Ray were in No. 912. The radio was on. The volume wasn't turned up, but in the empty suite, everything echoed. They didn't hear me come in.

I was going to take the gallon and leave. Cans of paint were all over the living room. The lid on the can I picked up wasn't on properly. Either Ray or Donny had pried it off, but instead of hammering it back down, they'd only set it in place. When I lifted the can, the lid came off. As I grabbed for it, the can tipped. Nearly the whole gallon poured out. Thick beige paint splattered down my pant leg, coating my shoe. It splashed across the drop sheet and spattered up the wall. Paint was everywhere. It soaked through to the parquet floor. By the time Ray came out of the bathroom, globs of honey beige oozed down the wall to the baseboards.

In the middle of Ray and I cleaning it up and arguing about whose fault it was, Malcolm walked in. We had paint halfway up our arms. Making sure not to step in it, Malcolm walked around us on his toes. "Wondered what was taking you so long, Mike." He went over to the window. Donny came out of the bedroom. He looked down at us. He chuckled. When he saw that Malcolm was there, he stopped. As he moved toward the window, Malcolm said over his shoulder, "Hey, Don. Long time no see."

Music echoed throughout the suite. Swearing under his breath, Ray sopped paint up as fast as he could, wringing the rag out over the paint can. Standing close to the glass, Donny and Malcolm were talking too softly for Ray and me to hear.

"What they're talking about?" Ray asked.

"I dunno." By the look of it, they weren't talking about anything in particular, but I wasn't even trying to hear. Donny shrugged a couple of times. Malcolm laughed and shook his head, disagreeing with whatever it was Donny was saying.

"Fuck!" Ray said, reaching for the last clean rag we had. He was anxious to get the mess cleaned up, quick. His shirt and pants were smeared with paint. He was making a bigger mess.

Out of the blue, Malcolm took a step back from the window. He made a fist and punched the glass. It shook.

Ray leaned back on his feet. "What are you guys doing?"

Malcolm put his shoulder against the window. As he pushed his weight into it, Ray laughed nervously. "You better be careful, Malcolm. It's a long way down."

Loud enough so Ray and me could hear him, Malcolm said, "Don't you know anything, Donny boy? The glass they build with nowadays, it's hard as concrete." He pounded the window harder, again and again. "It's bulletproof. I bet it's three layers thick."

There was a muffled *thump* each time Malcolm struck the window. As he hit it harder and harder, the glass vibrated, causing sunlight, our own reflections to ripple across its surface.

Donny stood, his back to Ray and me, looking out the window. Malcolm turned to face us.

Ray took his shirt off and used it to wipe up paint. Speaking louder than the radio so Ray and me could hear him, Malcolm said, "Donny boy here thinks I'm bullshitting. I told him the glass they put in these places could stop a fuckin' bull. It's got to. Think The Jordon's gunna take a chance with some pasty-white business man who comes back up to his suite after having a few too many at the Brass Rail? Stumbling around drunk? Look at the size of this glass." He made a sweeping motion toward the window.

"If he ever went through it, the place would be shut down like that." He snapped his fingers.

Ray looked for a clean rag. There weren't any. His voice cracked when he told Malcolm, "What about that guy, that office guy downtown who went through a window in one of those bank towers? Eh, what about him?"

Cracking his knuckles, Malcolm replied, "Urban myth. Never happened. People make that shit up all the time. Like alligators in sewers, or, or the guy who spends a night in a motel with a whore and wakes up with his kidney carved outta of him. None of that shit's true."

Malcolm looked at me. "Tell them, Mike. You're the big university man in the family. Go ahead, tell them. It's all bullshit."

Behind Malcolm, Donny asked, "Wanna bet?"

Instead of answering, Malcolm went into the kitchenette and turned the radio off.

"Did I hear you right?"

Donny held a folded twenty between his fingers. "Yeah, you heard me. Here's an *opportunity* for you to make twenty bucks."

Titling his head back, Malcolm said, "You wanna bet me that I'd be too chicken shit to run into the glass, soldier boy?" He went over beside Donny and spread his fingers, caressing the window. Taking a money clip out of the front pocket of his clean overalls, he pulled off a twenty and then another. "Forty. Double or nothing. What do you say, war hero?"

Donny took out another twenty, waving it under Malcolm's nose. Snatching the two bills, Malcolm said, "Ray can hold it. He's the boss man anyways."

Because Ray wasn't wearing his shirt anymore, Malcolm stuffed the bills into the pocket of my T-shirt.

Ray said, "Hang on. Hang on. Don't do anything stupid."

Even though he'd tried cleaning them, Ray's hands were coated in paint. Mine were, too. Both of us held our hands up, fingers pointed toward the ceiling like surgeons waiting to begin.

Stepping in the spilled paint, Malcolm came around behind Ray and me. He turned the brim of his painter's cap backward. Imitating a bull about to charge, he snorted and dragged one foot across the floor. With his shoulder leading, taking small steps, he rushed past us, directly toward Donny, nearly running over him. Donny didn't flinch. Malcolm hit the window.

Except for a *thump*, nothing happened. The window vibrated.

"See. An urban myth."

Ray sighed.

Donny scoffed, "Come on, you weren't goin' hard enough."

"How fuckin' hard did ya want me to go? Anyways, if you had been listening Rambo, the bet was, I'd run *into* the window, not *through* the window. What do ya think I am, a fuckin' idiot?" Malcolm turned his cap around so the brim was at the front.

"Ya, guess you're right, Malcolm." Like he was just goofing around, Donny shoved him, but not too hard. At least that's how it seemed from where I was.

As Malcolm stumbled backwards, his arms pin wheeling, his heel caught the edge of a drop cloth. He lost his balance and his shoulder struck the centre of the window. This time, he must have hit at a different angle. There was a cracking sound as the tempered glass smashed into thousands of tiny cubes. Fragmenting glass enclosed Malcolm like the window was absorbing him. For a few seconds, I couldn't see anything through the glass around him. It was like trying to see through frozen water. Then the glass vanished. Malcolm's arms spun faster. Then he was gone, too.

Gusts of humid air swirled around us. My ears popped. Someone screamed. People yelled. For the first time in the four months we'd been painting at The Jordon, sounds like horns and sirens, jackhammers and brakes screeching filled the suite.

Ray and I don't move. Tread marks from Malcolm's shoes in honey beige encircled us. I followed them with my eyes as far as the window where they stopped abruptly. All over the parquet glass shards glinted like crystals. Twisted lengths of the metal framing dangled from the sides and the ceiling.

Paint trickled down my wrist. Donny went to where the window had been and stood on the edge and leaned out. His hair blew off his face. Sucking air between his teeth, he shook his head. All he said was, "Shit."

Paint snaked down my arms, dripping from my elbows. Donny came and took the eighty dollars out of my pocket.

Opening his wallet, he carefully placed the bills inside.

"It was about time he left. He just needed a little—" Putting the wallet in his back pocket, Donny paused. He tugged his shirt cuffs down. He chuckled. "—he just needed a bit of encouragement, that's all."

Acknowledgments

I am indebted to Lidia Monaco for her support,
encouragement and trust. Lid, you've made this possible.

Thanks to Caroleen Brown; poofreader extraordinaire.

Members of the *Moosemeat Writing Group* (2003-2005).
Fellow writers, thank you for the critiques. I am honoured
to be counted amongst you.

Thank you Katharine King for your kind words.
Your depth of character is sincere.

Ken Murray in NYC. You respect the craft.
I admire this. Thank you.

Myna Wallin, for making the connection
and for putting me out front, I am grateful.

Catherine O'Toole read the final draft of *Playing Basra*
before submission. Her honesty was indispensable.
Her knowledge of the business, invaluable.

Special thanks to Exile's dedicated and skilled editor,
Chris Doda. Your recommendations brought the work
up to a brilliant shine.

Produced with the support of the City of Toronto
through a Toronto Arts Council grant.

This book is entirely printed on FSC certified paper.